Mason found a fresh diaper and tried grabbing the baby's ankles to raise her behind, but she kicked so hard it was tough to get a hold.

Settling for one ankle, he tried lifting her sideways, then sneaking the diaper under.

"Not like that," Hattie complained. Nudging Mason aside, she caught the baby's ankles one-handed on her first try.

"As much as it pains me to admit this," Mason said with a round of applause, "you're good."

"I've had at least a little practice. You'll get the hang of it." She took the diaper from him and, once she had it properly positioned, stepped aside for him to finish. "She's all yours."

When Mason stepped back, their arms brushed. The resulting hum of awareness caught him as off guard as practically flunking his first diapering lesson.

He and Hattie had never been more than friends, so what was that about? Had she felt it, too? If so, she showed no signs, which told him to just chalk it up to his imagination and get this job done.

Dear Reader,

At this point in my career, I don't often have the opportunity to inject much of my own life into my stories, but something in Hattie, this story's heroine, struck a chord in me I couldn't ignore. All my life, I've been what I now dub a professional dieter. I've tried every fad diet and weight loss system, from Weight Watchers to Nutrisystem to Jenny Craig. They all work for a week or two, but then old habits creep in, and I'm soon back to the weight where I started.

Hattie, too, has struggled her whole life with weight issues, so much so that when her dream guy puts the moves on her, she doesn't believe he could honestly fall for a girl like her—a "fat" girl. Well, navy SEAL Mason Brown isn't an ordinary guy, and he sure isn't so petty as to allow a few extra pounds keep him from admiring all the amazing qualities Hattie has to share.

Hattie helped me conquer a few of my own inner demons. And, while I'll never stop striving to fit into my size-ten college jeans, I now realize there's *way* more to life than dieting—like truly living and loving my wonderful friends and family!

I so hope you enjoy Hattie and Mason's story of second chances and new beginnings, and remember it's never too late to start a new beginning all your own!

Happy reading!

Laura Marie Altom

THE SEAL's CHRISTMAS TWINS

—

LAURA MARIE ALTOM

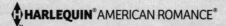
HARLEQUIN® AMERICAN ROMANCE®

Recycling programs
for this product may
not exist in your area.

ISBN-13: 978-0-373-75484-7

THE SEAL'S CHRISTMAS TWINS

Printed in U.S.A.

HARLEQUIN®
™ www.Harlequin.com

ABOUT THE AUTHOR

After college (Go, Hogs!), bestselling, award-winning author Laura Marie Altom did a brief stint as an interior designer before becoming a stay-at-home mom to boy-girl twins and a bonus son. Always an avid romance reader, she knew it was time to try her hand at writing when she found herself replotting the afternoon soaps.

When not immersed in her next story, Laura teaches art at a local middle school. In her free time, she beats her kids at video games, tackles Mount Laundry and, of course, reads romance!

Laura loves hearing from readers at either P.O. Box 2074, Tulsa, OK 74101, or by email, balipalm@aol.com.

Love winning fun stuff? Check out www.lauramariealtom.com.

Books by Laura Marie Altom

HARLEQUIN AMERICAN ROMANCE

1086—SAVING JOE*
1099—MARRYING THE MARSHAL*
1110—HIS BABY BONUS*
1123—TO CATCH A HUSBAND*
1132—DADDY DAYCARE
1147—HER MILITARY MAN
1160—THE RIGHT TWIN
1165—SUMMER LOVIN'
    "A Baby on the Way"
1178—DANCING WITH DALTON
1211—THREE BOYS AND A BABY
1233—A DADDY FOR CHRISTMAS
1257—THE MARINE'S BABIES
1276—A WEDDING FOR BABY**
1299—THE BABY BATTLE**
1305—THE BABY TWINS**
1336—THE BULL RIDER'S CHRISTMAS BABY***
1342—THE RANCHER'S TWIN TROUBLES***
1359—A COWGIRL'S SECRET***
1383—A BABY IN HIS STOCKING***
1415—A SEAL'S SECRET BABY‡
1430—THE SEAL'S STOLEN CHILD‡
1435—THE SEAL'S VALENTINE‡
1466—A NAVY SEAL'S SURPRISE BABY‡

*U.S. Marshals
**Baby Boom
***The Buckhorn Ranch
‡Operation: Family

This story is dedicated to my fellow "professional dieters." May someday soon scientists develop fat-free cheesecake that actually tastes of creamy, gooey goodness as opposed to cardboard!

Chapter One

"Wait—she's *dead?*" Navy SEAL Mason Brown covered his right ear so he could hear the caller. His team was at Virginia Beach's joint base, Fort Story, immersed in close quarters combat training. If his CO caught him on his cell, there'd be hell to pay. Just in case, he locked himself in a bathroom and crossed his fingers to not lose his already-shoddy signal. "Come again. I'm sure I didn't fully hear you."

"M-Mason, I'm sorry, but you heard me right. Melissa and Alec died. Their plane went down, and…" Hattie's voice was drowned out by the sort of electric, adrenaline-charged hum he usually only experienced at the height of combat. No way was this real. There had to be a mistake, because even though his ex-wife had betrayed him in the worst possible way, even though there'd been thousands of miles between them, he couldn't imagine life without her at least sharing the planet. "I'm sorry to break this to you over the phone, but with you so far away…"

"I get it." What he didn't get was his reaction. Melissa had cheated on him with his old pal Alec six years ago. So why had his limbs gone numb to the point he leaned against the closed bathroom door, sliding down, down until his carefully constructed emotional walls shattered, leaving him feeling raw and exposed and maybe even a little afraid.

"Mason, I know this is probably the last thing you want to hear at a time like this, but Melissa and Alec's lawyer needs to see you. He says you're in the will, and—"

"Why would I be in the will?" He clamped his hand to his forehead.

"I don't know. He wanted to call you, but I asked him to let me. I didn't want this kind of news coming from a stranger."

Isn't that essentially what we are? Though he and Hattie used to be tight, once he and Melissa split, Melissa had taken custody of the rest of her family, as well. In Divorce Land, wasn't that the natural order?

"Mason? Will you come?"

He groaned.

Just beyond the bathroom's far wall, gunfire popped like firecrackers. That was his world. Had been for a nice, long while and he felt comfortable here in Virginia. Back in his hometown of Conifer, Alaska, he was a pariah— which still burned his hide, considering he'd been the wounded party.

"Mason? I don't know why, but Melissa's lawyer's adamant you be present at the reading of her will."

Pop, pop, pop. Considering the fire knotting in his stomach, those shots might as well have been to his gut. "Yeah," he finally muttered. "I'll be there."

THURSDAY NIGHT, Hattie Beaumont volunteered for pickup duty. Her mother was too grief-stricken to leave her bed after having just lost her eldest daughter to a plane crash. Her dad wasn't faring much better. Glad to be inside and out of the blustery October wind, Hattie lugged her sister's five-month-old twins to the nearest row of chairs in Conifer's airport terminal—newly constructed after the old one collapsed following a heavy snowfall.

River-stone columns now supported the vaulted ceiling of the otherwise modest space that housed three regional airlines, two charter air companies, one rental-car agency, a coffee bar, sundries shop and diner.

At nine, everything was closed. Only three other parties waited for the night's last incoming flight from Anchorage.

The infants, finally sleeping in their carriers, had been heavy, but not near as heavy as the pain squeezing Hattie's heart.

Her sister Melissa's husband's twin-engine Cessna had gone down in bad weather on Tuesday. Alec died upon impact, but Melissa lived long enough for a search-and-rescue team to get her to an Anchorage hospital, where she'd passed Wednesday morning.

The realization that her sister was well and truly gone hadn't quite sunk in. It felt more like a nightmare from which she couldn't wake.

Alec's parents, Taylor and Cindy, understandably hadn't taken the news well. They'd retired in Miami, and it was their flight she was meeting. They planned to be in town until Saturday's double funeral. After that, Hattie wasn't sure of their plans—or anyone's plans for that matter. Would her parents and Alec's share custody of the twins?

Covering her face with her hands, Hattie fought a fresh wave of the nausea that she hadn't been able to shake since she'd first heard the news of Melissa's accident. Granted, people of all ages died all the time. Funerals were a sad fact of life, but having a close family member die didn't seem possible.

Then there was Mason…

Yeah. She'd table thoughts of him for another time. Too

much history. *Way* too much pain on top of an already-crushing amount of grief.

Steeling herself for her eventual reunion with him at her sister's funeral, then again at Sunday's reading of the will, Hattie was thankful that she wouldn't have to see him until then. Despite the fact that she'd had years apart from him to think of what she might say should she ever see him again, she still couldn't quite string together the words.

How was she supposed to act around the one guy she'd secretly adored? The guy who hadn't just gotten away, but had married and divorced her sister?

Minutes elongated into what felt like hours.

She tried playing a game on her phone but, after losing a dozen times, gave up.

Finally, the drone of the twin-engine Piper Chieftain taxiing to the passenger offloading area signaled the near-end of her grueling night. She doubted she'd even be able to sleep, but if she did, the break from reality would be most welcome.

She rose to wait for Alec's parents. Since the twins were still sleeping, she left them in the seating area that was only thirty feet from the incoming passengers' door.

"Hattie?"

She glanced to her left only to get a shock. Mason's dad, Jerry Brown, stood alongside her, holding out his arms for a hug. "Girl, it's been ages since I last saw you—though I hear you and Fern visit all the time."

"True. I can't get enough of her shortbread cookies." Fern was Jerry's neighbor. She was getting on in years, and Hattie enjoyed chatting with her. What she didn't enjoy was passing Mason's old house. The mere sight reminded her of happier times, which was why she hustled by, carefully avoiding a possible meeting with Jerry. The last thing she wanted was to hear about his son. For hearing about

Mason would only serve as a reminder of how much he was missed.

He laughed. "That makes two of us." His smile faded. "Addressing the elephant in the room, how're you and your folks coping? Both your sister and Alec gone…" He shook his head. "One helluva blow."

"Yeah." She swallowed back tears. "I'm here to pick up Alec's parents."

"I'm grabbing Mason. It'll be damn good to see him, though I wish our visit was under happier circumstances."

Mason will be here? Now? As in the next thirty seconds?

Considering her sister had just died, fashion hadn't topped her priorities. Hattie wore jeans, a faded Green Bay Packers sweatshirt a patron had left at her bar, and she'd crammed her hair into a messy bun—as for makeup, it hadn't even occurred to her. *Jeez, what is wrong with you? Why are you worried about how you look?*

She shook her head, suddenly feeling jittery.

Sure, she'd known Mason would be coming for the funeral, but she'd assumed they wouldn't run into each other until Saturday. This was too soon. What would she say or do?

Whereas moments earlier grief had slowed her pulse, panic now caused it to race. She couldn't see him. Not yet.

And then an airline representative stole all options for possible escape by opening the doors. In strode Mason. Out went her last shred of confidence.

She took a few steps back into a shadow. With luck, Mason wouldn't even see her.

The plan proved simple, yet effective, as Mason and his dad were soon caught up in their reunion.

Two strangers entered the terminal, and then Alec's parents. What were their thoughts about Mason having been on their flight? Or were they so absorbed in their grief, they hadn't noticed?

"Cindy? Taylor?" Hattie waved them over. "Hi. How was your flight?"

Cindy's eyes appeared red and sunken, her expression hollow. Taylor didn't look much better.

"It was fine," Taylor said, "but we're ready to call it a day."

"I understand. Should I get a cart for your luggage?"

He shook his head. "We don't have much."

"Okay, well…I'll grab the twins, and we'll be on our way." *Awkward* didn't begin to describe the moment, especially when she accidentally glanced in Mason's direction, but he turned away. Purposely? She hoped not.

SUNDAY AFTERNOON MASON shoveled for all he was worth, but still couldn't keep up with the mid-October snow. Located on the eastern shore of Prince William Sound, Conifer was known for impressive snowfalls. As an oblivious kid, he'd spent hours happily building forts and snowmen and, if he'd been really ambitious, even tunnels. Now he needed to dig out his dad's old truck, carefully avoiding the passenger-side door, which was barely attached to the vehicle after it had been rammed by an angry plow driver some ten years earlier.

His dad's trailer was dwarfed by towering Sitka spruce. Mason used to like playing hide-and-seek in them. Now, having grown used to the open sea, the dark forest made him feel trapped.

It had been six long years since he'd been home.

Best as he could remember, he'd once enjoyed the whisper of wind through the boughs. Today, the world had fallen silent beneath the deepening blanket of snow. If pressed, he'd have to admit the evergreen and ice-laced air smelled damned good. Fresh and clean—the way his life used to be.

"This is the last place I expected to see you."

"Same could be said of you." Mason glanced toward the familiar voice to find little Hattie Beaumont all grown up. He'd seen her in the airport when he'd come in, but with Alec's parents having been there, the timing was all wrong for any kind of meaningful conversation. That morning, at the funeral, hadn't been much better. "Not a great day for an afternoon stroll."

"I like it." At the funeral, he'd been so preoccupied, he hadn't fully absorbed the fact that the former tomboy had matured into a full-on looker. She was part Inuit, and the snow falling on her long dark hair struck him as beautiful. Her brown eyes lacked her usual mischievous sparkle, but then, given the circumstances, he supposed that was to be expected. "Feels good getting out of the house."

"Agreed." He rested his gloved hands on the shovel's handle. "Snow expected to stop anytime soon?"

"Mom says we could see ten inches by morning."

"Swell." Around here, pilots flew through just about anything Mother Nature blew their way, but a major storm could put a kink in his plans to fly out first thing in the morning.

"We still on for this afternoon?"

He nodded. "Two, right?"

"Yes. Benton's opening his office just for us, so don't be late."

He couldn't help but grin. "Little Hattie Beaumont, who never once made it to school on time, is lecturing me on punctuality? And how many nights did your mother send me out to find you for dinner?"

Eyes shining, she looked away from him, then smiled. "Good times, huh?"

"The best." Back then, he'd had it all figured out. Perfect woman, job—even had his eye on a fixer-upper at the lonely end of Juniper Lane. Considering how tragic his parents' marriage had ultimately been, he should've known better than to believe his life would turn out any different.

Joining the navy had been the best thing he'd ever done.

"Well…" She gestured to the house next door. "I wanted to thank Fern for the pies and ham she brought to the wake. Might as well check her firewood while I'm there."

"Want me to tag along?" He'd forgotten the spirit of community up here. The way everyone watched out for everyone else. He'd lived in his Virginia Beach apartment for just over five years, but still didn't have a clue about any of his neighbors.

"Thanks, but I can handle it." Her forced smile brought on a protective streak in him for the girl who'd grown into a woman.

"I'm not saying you can't. Just offering to lend a hand. Besides…" Half smiling, he shook his head. "I haven't seen Fern since she ratted me out for driving my snowmobile across her deck."

"She still hasn't built railings. I'm surprised nobody's tried it since."

"What can I say? I'm an original."

"More like a delinquent." She waved goodbye and walked down the street, then shouted, "Don't be late!"

"I won't."

"Oh—and, Mason?" He'd resumed shoveling, but looked up to find her biting her lower lip.

"Yeah?"

She looked down. "Thanks for coming. I really appreciate it."

"Sure. No problem," he lied. Actually, returning to Conifer had brought on an unfathomable amount of pain. Remembering Hattie's big sister, Melissa—the love of his life—was never easy. Not only had she broken his heart, but spirit. She'd taught him *trust* should've been a four-letter word. He hated her on a scale he'd thought himself incapable of reaching.

Now that she was dead?

All that hate mixed with guilt culminated in killer heartburn and an insatiable need to escape.

Chapter Two

Hattie had believed her childhood crush on Mason long over. Then he'd gone and flashed his crooked smile, opening the gate for her flood of feelings for him to come rushing back.

Along with her parents—the twins were being watched by their neighbor Sophie—Hattie now sat outside the office of family friend, and the only lawyer in town, Benton Seagrave, waiting for Mason to arrive. The metal folding chair serving as his trailer's bare-bones reception area made her squirmy. The scent of burnt coffee churned her stomach.

As with many folks in Alaska, Benton had a personal drive outside of his profession. He practiced law from October through May—and then, begrudgingly. His summers were spent on his gold claim in the Tolovana-Livengood region. The only reason he'd agreed to see the family today was because Mason and Alec's folks flew out in the morning.

Holding her hands clasped on her knees, Hattie closed her eyes, contrasting her remembered images of Mason with ones recently gained.

He'd always been taller than her, but now she felt positively petite standing beside him—not an easy feat for a woman a few local teens still called Fattie Hattie. Not only had he grown in height, but stature. He'd shoveled in his

Sorel boots, jeans and a brown long-johns top that had clung to broadened shoulders and pecs. When he'd shoveled, his biceps could've earned their own zip code. Sure, in the bar she owned plenty of fit men came and went, but none caused her stomach to somersault with just a flash of a crooked smile. Mason's blue eyes had darkened and lines now creased the corners. His perpetually mussed dark hair shone with golden highlights. She was two years younger than him, and while the few other kids they'd gone to school with mercilessly teased her about her weight, he'd actually talked to her, sharing her love of astronomy and fishing and most of all…her sister.

On Mason and Melissa's wedding day, Hattie had tried being happy, but in actuality, she'd suffered through, forcing her smile and well-wishes, secretly resenting her sister for not only her too-tight maid-of-honor dress selection, but for marrying the only man Hattie had ever loved.

Of course in retrospect, Hattie knew she hadn't loved Mason, but crushed on him. Daydreamed of him holding her, kissing her, declaring it had never been Melissa he'd wanted, but her. Now that Melissa was dead, the mere thought of those traitorous longings made her feel dirty and disrespectful.

Melissa was—had been—the bronzed beauty every guy wanted. For as long as she could remember, Hattie battled jealousy and resentment she'd never wanted, but seemed to have always carried. When Melissa destroyed Mason by cheating on him, well, Hattie had secretly sided with him in believing her own sister heartless and cruel. Years later, when Melissa struggled to conceive, Hattie's guilt doubled for believing her sister's infertility was karma paying a call.

Now that Melissa was dead, self-loathing consumed Hattie for not only all of that, but not being able to cry.

Since the accident, she'd been the strong one, shielding her parents from the painful process of burying their perfect child, their pretty child, the one their Inuit mother had called *piujuq*—beautiful.

From outside came the clang of someone mounting the trailer's metal steps. Seconds later, the door was tugged open. Mason ducked as he entered, brushing snow from his dark hair. He still wore his jeans and boots, but had added an ivory cable-knit sweater that made his blue eyes all the more striking. For a moment, Hattie fell speechless. Then she remembered she wasn't seeing Mason for a happy reunion, but the reading of her sister's will.

Her parents, still holding tight to their resentment over the divorce—and especially his attendance at an intimate family moment such as the reading of Melissa's will—barely acknowledged his presence.

"Am I late?" He checked his black Luminox watch, the kind she'd seen on divers around town. Certain times of year, Conifer was a bustling port.

"W-we're early." She struggled knowing what to do with her hands. "Alec's parents should be here soon, so Benton said to let him know when we're all ready."

"Sure." Mason shoved his hands in his pockets.

And then they waited.

No one said a word. Aside from wind gusts and papery whispers of *Reader's Digest* pages being turned, all in the cramped space had fallen silent. Thank goodness Hattie's racing thoughts and pulse had no volume or everyone would know the extent of her panic. For years, she'd dreamed of a reunion with Mason, but never under these circumstances.

Twenty minutes passed with still no sign of Alec's parents.

A muffled landline rang in Benton's office, then came a brief, equally muffled conversation.

"Look," Mason said, "if you all don't mind, I'd just as soon get started. I can't imagine what Melissa would've left me. The whole thing's bizarre."

"Agreed," Hattie's father said, also rising, offering his hand to his wife. Akna and Lyle led the way down the short hall leading to Benton's office.

Before Lyle had reached the door, Benton opened it. "Good, you're all here." He waved Akna and Lyle into the room. "That was Taylor and Cindy on the phone. They're not going to make it."

"Everything all right?" Lyle asked.

"As well as can be expected."

While her parents and Benton made polite conversation, Hattie hung back with Mason. He made the formerly smallish space feel cramped. She needed to get away from him. And take time to process what losing her sister really meant.

"Ladies first." He gestured for her to lead the way, which was the last thing she wanted. She felt most comfortable in jeans and a roomy sweatshirt. Her black slacks and plum sweater clung in all the wrong places and she'd never wished more for a ponytail holder to hold her long hair from her face.

The graying lawyer greeted them at the door, shaking their hands. "Damn sorry about all this. Melissa and Alec were good people."

Really? The weight of what her sister and Mason's former best friend had done hung heavy in the room.

Her parents had already been seated.

Mason cleared his throat. "I don't mean to be rude, but can we get on with this?"

Hattie sympathized with what he must be going through.

Just as she had guilt, he must harbor anger. Granted, Mason had left Conifer years ago and his absence no doubt tempered the initial sting of finding his wife in bed with his best friend, but there wasn't a statute of limitations on that sort of thing. Hattie couldn't imagine how Mason now felt regarding the lovebirds' sudden deaths.

Benton's office could've been featured on a special episode of *Hoarders*. Stacks upon stacks of files leaned precariously on every available surface.

Behind his desk, Benton shuffled through three more leaning piles. He tugged one out, only to have the whole pile follow in a paper-work avalanche. "Oops." He flashed them all a reassuring smile. "Happens all the time. Give me a sec, and we'll be back on course. Hattie, Mason, please, have a seat."

Mason knelt to assist with the cleanup.

Normally, Hattie would've helped, too, but at the moment, she lacked the strength.

"There we go," Benton finally said, reassembling the file he'd previously held. "Thanks, Mason."

"No problem."

"All right, then, let's skip formalities and get right to the meat of the matter."

"Perfect." Lyle took Akna's hand.

Hattie wished for someone to comfort her.

Two additional padded folding chairs faced Benton's desk. Mason sat in the one nearest the window.

Hattie took the other.

To Hattie, Benton said, "Having Vivian and Vanessa changed your sister—softened her to a degree I'm not sure she allowed most people to see."

Resting his elbows on his knees, Mason grunted.

Hattie commenced with squirming, carefully avoiding brushing against Mason in the too-close space.

"She was highly superstitious about Alec's flying. After their marriage, he had me write up a will, stating her his sole beneficiary."

Sighing, Mason asked, "What does any of that have to do with me?"

Hattie pressed her lips tight to keep from saying something she might regret. Mason had a right to be angry with Melissa, but he didn't have to be rude. Even though Hattie had her own issues with her sister, when it came down to it, she'd loved her as much as everyone else had in their small town. Melissa's beauty and spirit had been irresistible. Their parents hadn't been upset with their eldest for having an affair. Instead, they'd believed Mason—formerly a commercial fisherman—in the wrong for being gone so many days at sea, especially at a time when she'd needed him more than ever.

The lawyer closed the file and sighed. "I'm afraid this has everything to do with you, Mason—quite literally. Alec left the entirety of his estate to Melissa…."

Akna held a tissue to her nose. "Please, hurry."

"Of course." Benton consulted the file. "Bottom line, Melissa bequeathed everything to Hattie and Mason in the event both she and Alec passed at the same time."

"What?" Lyle released Akna to stand. "That's ridiculous."

"Surely, not everything—not…the girls?" Tears streamed down Akna's weathered cheeks.

Benton nodded. "Afraid so."

"Why?" Hattie asked.

"This might explain." He handed a letter to Mason, but Mason held up his hands. "You read it. I don't want anything to do with any of this."

Akna shot him a dark look.

"Very well…" Benton took the sealed letter, opened it, then began to read.

"Mason—
If you're reading this, my dreams were indeed the premonition I'd feared. I know you never held much faith in my Inuit heritage, but we place great significance on dreams, and as I have had the same dream of Alec and me passing on three different occasions, I feel compelled to make arrangements should the worst indeed happen.

First, I owe you an apology. Our losing the baby was a horrible accident, nothing either of us could've prevented. I'm sorry I not only blamed the miscarriage on you, but was too cowardly to admit I'd outgrown our relationship."

Mason stood, hand over his mouth, eyes shining with unshed tears.

Benton asked, "Would you like to read the rest in private?"

"Get it over with." Hands clenching into fists, Mason stared out the window on the far side of the room.

"You're a monster," Akna said. "How dare you disrespect my daughter's last words."

"Honey…" Lyle slipped his arms about her shoulders.

Hattie wished for an escape hatch to open beneath her chair.

Benton cleared his throat, then continued to read from the letter.

"I'm ashamed to admit, my whole life was spent in the pursuit of pleasure. Now that I'm a parent, I understand how much more to life there is. Honor and self-sacrifice. The kinds of traits I now recognize not only in my sister and parents, but you.

I doubt you're aware of this, but Hattie has harbored quite the crush on you for as long as she could walk well enough to follow you around. If my dreams are true, and I am soon to die, I want to do something well and truly good.

The best thing I can think of is to play matchmaker. If you and Hattie end up together, not only will my gorgeous twins end up with a great set of parents, but my beautiful, kindhearted sister will live happily ever after with the good guy she's always deserved.

"That's it." Benton folded the note, returning it to the envelope. "Lyle, Akna, I hope that answers your questions as to why your daughter chose to leave her twins to Hattie and Mason."

"We'll contest it." Akna held a white-knuckled grip on her purse. "My grandbabies need to be with me. Family."

"Wh-what am I?" Hattie managed past the wall of tears blocking her throat.

"Your mother didn't mean it like that," Lyle assured her.

"Lord almighty…" While the wind howled outside the trailer's paper-thin walls and windows, Mason shook his head. "I feel like we've been here ten days. This is nuts. No one gives away kids based on a few stupid dreams."

Akna fired off a round of Inuit curses at Mason.

Hattie's chest had tightened. As much as she adored her baby nieces, in no way, shape or form was she ready to become a mom. Melissa had tossed around formally naming Hattie as the twins' godmother a few times, but that'd been just talk. Hattie had always dreamed of being a mom, but considering her lackluster social life, she'd resigned herself to the fact that unless Prince Charming breezed in on a white snowmobile, her only destiny was to become an old maid. She couldn't even process the fact that her sister had just outed her feelings for Mason.

"No." Mason paced the cramped, sterile office. "I want no part of this. Clearly, Melissa wasn't in her right mind, and I sure as hell don't believe Inuit dream voodoo."

"You hush!" Akna demanded.

Hattie shot him a look. "Leave my culture out of this." Of Benton, she asked, "Are you sure Melissa didn't want the girls to be with their grandparents? My mom and dad have already taken them in."

"As you heard in not just the letter, but on all legal documentation, Melissa was quite clear in her wishes. She wanted the girls raised in their own home by her sister and her ex-husband."

Mason snorted. "Look, I can tell you right now this isn't happening. I'm due back on base first thing Tuesday morning, and want no part of Melissa's twisted matchmaking scheme—no offense, Hattie. You're a great gal, but…"

"I get it," she said, mortified her own sister would stoop so low as to embarrass her from beyond the grave.

Benton said, "It's understandable you'd need a few days to adjust to something of this nature."

"There's no adjusting. Deal me out."

Hattie glanced over her shoulder to find Mason's complexion lightened by a couple shades. He'd narrowed his eyes and held the heels of his hands to his forehead.

"Hattie?" Benton asked. "How do you feel regarding the matter?"

She straightened, drawing strength from not only herself, but her ancestors. "If this is what Melissa wanted for her children, who am I to deny her? Not sure how," she said with a faint laugh, "but I will raise my nieces."

"This is wrong," Akna said.

"I agree." Lyle shifted on his seat. "Weren't there other letters from our daughter? Why'd she leave just the one?"

Benton rifled through the file. "That appears to be the only one. She gave me the packet herself. Before now, I never checked the contents. But, Hattie, if you feel capable of raising your nieces, there's no reason Mason should feel compelled to stay."

"Good." Mason now rested his hands on his hips. "Perfect solution. The kids are in capable hands, and I'm back on my base. Problem solved."

"Not so fast." The lawyer wagged a pen. "Mason, while I understand your reluctance to take on such a challenge, as of now, you and Hattie share legal custody of Vivian and Vanessa. A family-court judge can release you from this responsibility, but it will take time."

A muscle ticked in Mason's clenched jaw. "How much time are we talking?"

"Well, let's see…" Benton took a few endless minutes to consult his computer. "Ironically, the nearest family-court judge for five hundred miles is on maternity leave. A judge in Valdez is temporarily hearing her cases. First thing Monday morning, Mason, I'll get you on Judge Dvorck's docket, but considering the fact that, like it or not, Melissa's twins are your legal responsibility, I'd strongly advise you to assume their care until the judge releases you from all financial and custodial ties to the estate." Withdrawing a legal-sized envelope from his top desk drawer, he opened it, then passed along two sets of keys. "These belong to Melissa and Alec's home and cars. Counting real estate, life insurance and investments, the twins—and you—should live quite comfortably." He gave Mason and Hattie each copies of the files. "These contain detailed listings of all assets."

Hattie felt near drowning. Was this real?

Her mother quietly sobbed.

Lyle helped his wife to her feet. "Let's go. It's clear we're not needed."

Damn Melissa for doing this to their parents.

"So wait—" Mason said once Lyle and Akna had gone. "Me and Hattie are supposed to drag Melissa's kids from their grandparents, then camp out at Alec and Melissa's house until we see the judge?"

"That's about the size of it. Any further questions?" Benton raised his considerable eyebrows.

Oh—Hattie had plenty more she needed to know, but for the moment, the most pressing issue was how was she supposed to keep her sanity while playing *house* with stupid-handsome Mason?

Chapter Three

In the time they'd spent with Benton, the weather had turned from pretty lightly falling snow to downright blowing ugly. The trailer's grated-steel stairs were snow-covered and treacherous. This time of year, on a clear, bright day they only had maybe ten hours of sun. During the two hours they'd been inside, darkness had settled in.

Mason held out his hand to Hattie, who stood behind him. "Let me help."

"I'm fine!" she said above the wind.

Ignoring her, he took firm hold of her arm. "You won't make it five feet in those heels. Forget you live in Alaska?"

When she struggled to escape him, common sense took over and he scooped her into his arms.

"Put me down!"

He did—once he'd reached her SUV. "There you go. I'll follow you to your folks'. I'm assuming that's where the twins currently reside?"

"Not necessary. I'll take it from here."

"Why are you being so stubborn?"

She ignored him to fish through her purse for her keys, which she promptly dropped in the snow.

They both knelt at the same time and ended up conking heads.

"Ouch," they said in unison, rubbing their noggins.

Mason had to laugh. "This reminds me of that time I took you salmon fishing and you damn near knocked yourself out just leaving the boat's cabin."

"I tripped and you know it."

"Yeah, yeah…" He found her keys, then pressed the remote. "Climb in. I'll see you in a few."

"Mason…"

Her dark, wary tone told him she'd prefer he stay away, but he'd never been one to shirk duty and didn't plan on starting now. For whatever time he was legally charged with caring for Melissa's kids, he would. Out of the memory of what they'd once shared, he owed her that much.

The storm made it tough to see the road, but Mason was familiar enough with the route to his former in-laws' he could've driven it blindfolded. He'd shared a lot of good times with Melissa and Hattie's parents. This afternoon, like the day of Melissa's funeral, wouldn't be one.

The back-and-forth drone of the wipers transported him to another snowy day. Weeks after his divorce had been finalized, he'd been fresh off the boat from a grueling two-month Yakutat king-crab season to find himself with his dad at the Juniper Inn's Sunday brunch seated two tables down from newlyweds Melissa and Alec. As if that weren't bad enough, Akna and Lyle were also in attendance. As long as he lived, he'd never forget their disapproving stare. Melissa's betrayal—and Alec's—had been hard enough to bear.

His dad counseled to play it cool. Not to let them get beneath his skin. They weren't worth it. But all through middle and high school, throughout his and Melissa's two-year marriage, he'd loved Akna and Lyle. They were good people. It killed him to think for one second they blamed him for his marriage falling apart. Yes, he'd spent a lot of time away from home, but he was working for Melissa—them. Their future.

Losing their baby hadn't been anyone's fault.

He remembered a fire crackling in the inn's too-fussy dining room. His chair had been too straight-backed and uptight. Even though the weather outside was bitterly cold, inside struck him as annoyingly hot. As long as he lived, he'd never forget the way the snow pelting the windows melted on contact, running in tearlike rivulets that reminded him of Melissa's tears when she'd asked for a divorce.

She'd claimed his distance had driven her to Alec—not physical distance, but emotional. She'd said the miscarriage changed him. Mason believed that a crock. She was the one who'd changed. His love had never once faltered.

On autopilot, back in the present, he parked his dad's old pickup in front of Akna and Lyle's house.

Though the temperature had dropped to the teens, his palms were sweating. Countless dangerous SEAL missions had left him less keyed up.

Hattie pulled into her parents' driveway ahead of him. She now teetered on their front-porch steps. What'd gotten into her? The Hattie he remembered struck him as a practical, no-frills girl who knew better than to wear high-heel boots in a snowstorm. But then, that girl had also been a tomboy, doe-eyed dreamer who'd preferred the company of her dogs over most people. It saddened him to realize he no longer knew the striking woman she'd grown into. They might as well be strangers.

She damn near tripped, so he hastened his pace to a jog.

"Slow it down." He took her arm. "You act like this is somewhere you want to be."

Wrenching her arm free, she grasped the railing instead of him. "Where else would I be? This is my family. Used to be yours."

He snorted.

At seventeen, he and Hattie had helped Lyle build this porch over a warm summer weekend. Melissa had sat in a lawn chair, *supervising*. Over ten years later, the wood groaned beneath their footfalls. Bitter wind whistled through the towering conifers that had given the town its name.

The front door popped open. Lyle ushered his daughter inside. "Hurry, it's cold. Your mom and I were just wondering what took so—" He eyed Mason. "What're you doing here?"

"Nice to see you, too." Mason trailed after Hattie, easing past her father. In the tiled entry, he brushed snow from his hair.

Hattie bustled with the busy work of removing her coat, then taking his.

Took about two seconds for Mason to assess his surroundings well enough to realize he'd stumbled deep into enemy territory.

Akna sat on one end of the sofa holding an infant wrapped in a pink blanket. Sophie Reynolds—a buxom busybody he remembered as being a neighbor and clerk down at Shamrock's Emporium—held another pink bundle in a recliner. Despite a cheery fire, the room struck Mason as devoid of warmth. As if the loss of their child had sucked the life from Hattie's parents.

Unsure what to say or even what to do with his hands, Mason crossed his arms. "Brutal out there."

Akna flashed a hollow-eyed stare briefly in his direction, before asking her daughter, "I suppose you're here for the girls?"

"Mom…" Hattie leaned against the wall while unzipping one boot, then the other. "Honestly? You probably need some rest. And it's not like you can't see the twins as often as you like."

Sophie noted, "A body can never see too much of their grandbabies."

Mason didn't miss Hattie's narrow-eyed stare in Sophie's direction.

While Mason stood rooted in the entryway, Hattie joined her mother on the sofa, taking the baby into her arms. Her tender reverence reminded him that Alec had been the one who'd ultimately given Melissa her most cherished desire. Part of him felt seized by childish, irrational jealousy over his once best friend filling his wife's need for babies. But then the grown-up in him took over, reminding Mason the point was moot, considering both parties were dead.

"It's not the same, and you know it." Akna angled on the sofa, facing her daughter and granddaughter. "Right, Sophie?"

Sophie nodded. "Amen."

Akna said, "Your sister betrayed me." By rote, she made the sign of the cross on her chest. The official family religion had always been an odd pairing of old Inuit ways blended with Lyle's Catholicism. A gold-framed photo of the Pope hung alongside Melissa's and Hattie's high school graduation pictures.

"Oh, stop. Melissa loved you very much." Hattie's voice cracked, causing Mason to shift uncomfortably. As much as he'd told himself he hated Melissa, wanted her to hurt as badly as she'd hurt him, he'd never wanted this. Hattie regained her composure. She'd always been the stronger of the two sisters.

"Obviously, not enough. And how could she have ignored Alec's parents? When your father called to tell them the news, poor Cindy had a breakdown. Taylor's got them on the first flight out in the morning so she can see her doctor."

"Such a shame," Sophie murmured.

"Akna, I'm sorry about all this." Mason left the entry to join them. "Which is why—soon as possible—I'll sign over my rights to Hattie. What you all do from there is your business."

"Hattie," Akna asked, "with the time you spend at the bar, do you even feel capable of raising twins?"

Hattie shrugged before tracing the back of her finger along her sleeping niece's cheek. "If this is what Melissa wanted, I feel honor bound to at least try."

Lyle ran his hands through his hair and sighed. "A few weeks ago, Melissa and the girls rode along with me while I covered for one of my delivery guys." A former bush pilot, Lyle now owned a grocery distribution center that served many nearby small communities. "Looking back, she acted jumpy. She mentioned not having been sleeping. Didn't think much of it at the time—chalked it up to her being a new mom. She talked a lot about wanting Hattie to be the girls' godmother, and that if something ever happened to her, she wanted them raised young."

"What does that even mean?" Akna asked through the tissue she'd held to her nose.

"Ask me, this is all unnatural," Sophie said. "The girls should be with their grandparents who love them."

Hattie ignored the neighbor and forced a deep breath. "Mom, no offense to you and Dad, but Melissa brought up the godmother thing with me, too. At the time, I told her she was talking crazy, but she said she wanted the girls raised by someone young. I guess her friend Bess was taken in by her grandmother, then lost her, which is how she ended up in foster care until she turned eighteen. Melissa didn't want that for her girls."

"We'd never let that happen," Lyle said.

Hattie took her niece from Akna's arms. "Look, I know this is a shock for everyone—me, too—but if this is what Melissa wanted—"

Her mother interjected, "What about *our* wishes?"

Lyle sat beside his wife, taking her hand. "Honey, what we want doesn't matter. All we can do is support Hattie as best we can."

"I would be calling a lawyer," Sophie said.

"Sophie," Hattie said, "please, stay out of this family matter. And, Mom, I don't mean to be harsh, but you're acting petty." Standing, Hattie cupped her hand to the infant's head. Hattie's brown eyes narrowed the way they always had when she dug in her heels to fight for what she wanted. "Why can't we raise the twins together? As of now, Mason and I might have legal custody, but what does that really even mean? I'll move into Melissa and Alec's, which is—what?—three miles from you? You used to watch the girls all the time for Melissa and Alec. Won't you do the same now for me? Vivian and Vanessa will be raised in the only home they've known, by people they love. I fail to see how this isn't the best all-around solution—especially since Mason already agreed to take himself out of the equation."

"It isn't the best," Sophie said, "because grandparents are best. You've never been around little ones. How will you even know what to do?"

While Sophie, in her infinite wisdom, rattled on, Mason was unprepared for the personal sting he felt at Hattie's speech. Did she have to make him sound so heartless and uncaring? But what else could he do? He had no stake in these little lives. Prior to their parents' funeral, he'd never even seen the girls. If he had his way, he'd be on a return flight to Virginia first thing in the morning.

Akna had been silently crying, but her pain now turned to uncontrollable sobbing. "Wh-why did this h-happen?"

Lyle slipped his arm around her.

Sophie closed her eyes in prayer.

Mason felt emotionally detached from the scene, as if he were watching a movie. What was he doing here? This was no longer his life.

Sophie abruptly stood. The once-sleeping infant she'd cradled was startled by the sudden movement and whimpered.

"Here, Mr. Mom." She thrust the baby into his arms. "You think yourself an expert, take over."

Mason didn't even know which baby he held, let alone what to do when her fitful protest turned into a full-blown wail.

THIRTY MINUTES LATER, Hattie held Vanessa with her right arm, struggling to unlock her sister and brother-in-law's former home. Mason stood behind her with Vivian, who hadn't stopped crying since leaving her grandparents.

"She always like this?" Mason set the bulging diaper bag on the porch.

"Usually, they're both easygoing, but it's been a rough couple days—for everyone."

"Yeah."

She finally got the key turned and opened the door on a house cold and dark and lonely enough to have been a tomb. When Melissa and Alec had been alive, the A-frame log cabin glowed with warmth and laughter. Her sister had been a wonderful cook and she'd always had something delicious baking or bubbling in one of her cast-iron pots.

The storm had passed and the two-story living room

featured a glass wall looking out on all of Treehorn Valley and Mount Kneely beyond. Moonlight reflecting off the snow cast a frosty bluish pallor over what Hattie knew to be warm-toned pine furniture upholstered in a vibrant red-orange and yellow *inukshuk* pattern.

"Cold in here." Mason closed the door with his foot. "Think the furnace is out?"

"Probably. It's a wood-burning system with propane backup. The temperature's been so mild, Alec probably didn't have it going for the season yet."

"Is it downstairs?"

She nodded, wandering through the open space, turning on lamps and overhead lights.

"I'll check it out, but in the meantime, what do you want me to do with this one?" He nodded at still-sniffling and red-eyed Vivian.

"I'll take her." Melissa kept a playpen in the warmest kitchen corner. Hattie set Vanessa in it, then took Vivian. Since the air was cold enough to see her breath, she kept the girls' outerwear on while she made a fire in the living room's river-stone hearth.

Being in her sister's home without Melissa unnerved her. Hattie normally occupied the one-bedroom efficiency apartment above her waterfront bar. It was small, cramped and cozy. Just the way she liked it. This space was too large for her taste. Though beautifully decorated in what she supposed was the classic Alaskan hunting lodge look, featuring an antler chandelier and an oil painting of snowcapped Mount Kneely over the mantel, this was her sister's dream house—not hers. Hattie thrived among clutter.

The house shuddered when the sleeping furnace lumbered awake.

A few minutes later when warm air flowed through the vents, gratitude swelled in Hattie for Mason handling at least that issue. She would've eventually gotten the unit started, but having one less worry was welcome.

Vivian fussed, reaching for her hat.

"I know, sweetie, it's annoying, but until it warms up in here, let's keep it on, okay?" Hattie knelt before the play-pen, patting the infant's back.

Mason's boots clomped on the hardwood stairs. "Alec has enough wood to last the week, so as long as one of us remembers to feed the beast, we'll at least be warm for the time being. Before winter sets in, though, I'll have to stockpile a legit supply. I'll make a fire up here, too."

"Already did, but it probably needs stoking."

Both babies were back to fussing. Were they hungry?

Hands to her throbbing forehead, Hattie wished she'd taken more than a casual interest in her nieces. Playing with them had been a much higher priority than an activity as mundane as meals. Hattie knew Melissa had breastfed, supplemented by formula, but the exact powder-to-water ratio escaped her.

"Since I'm over here, handling man work," Mason said from the hearth, "how about you do something about the kids' racket?"

"Love to, but it's gonna take a sec to get the formula mixed."

By the time Hattie finished, dancing firelight banished the living room's dark corners, but did little to ease the pain in her heart.

Both babies still fussed, which only made her fumble more. At the bar, she thrived under the chaotic pressure of a busy Friday or Saturday night. This was different.

"Need help?" Behind her, Mason hovered. His radiated heat further unnerved her. The situation was already be-yond horrible. Tossing her old high school crush into the mix only made matters worse. And here she'd thought

Melissa and Mason's wedding had been hard? This was a thousand times tougher.

"Sure." She managed to swallow past the emotional brick lodged in her throat. "You take Vanessa and a bottle and I'll grab Vivian."

In front of the playpen, he scratched his head. "Love to do just that, only I don't have a clue which one is Vanessa."

"You'll learn. Although there are still times I'm not sure, Vanessa typically has a more laid-back disposition. Vivian has no trouble letting you know she's displeased."

As if she knew her aunt was talking smack about her, Vivian upped the volume on her wail.

He snorted. "Sounds like you and your sister."

For the first time since the funeral, Hattie genuinely smiled. "Never thought of it like that, but you nailed your assessment—which makes me an awful person, right?"

"Not even close," he said over the infant's cry. "Melissa was a handful and were she here with us, she'd be first to admit it—with a proud smile."

"True."

When they each cradled an infant, they settled on the sofa in front of the fire.

Hattie plucked off the twins' hats and mittens, then gave Vivian her bottle. The sudden silence save for the fire's crackle and the twins' occasional grunts and sighs made for much-welcomed peace.

"Sorry about what happened at my parents'. That was an ugly scene."

"No worries." He shifted Vanessa to hold her in the crook of his other arm. "I don't blame them for being upset—Alec's folks, too. They've got to be feeling out of the loop."

"I suppose. But it doesn't have to be that way. They're

welcome to see these two whenever they'd like. They chose to run back to Florida."

"I know, but think of this from their perspective. Alec used to be my best friend, then I caught him sleeping with my wife and never spoke to him again. Cindy and Taylor were like second parents to me. Growing up, I ate more dinners at their house than mine. Everything's so mixed up, you know? Part of me was glad to see them at the funeral—at least until I remembered they were part of the enemy team. I imagine they feel the same?"

"Probably." Vivian had thankfully drifted off to sleep. Hattie gently leaned forward, setting the empty bottle on the coffee table. "Wonder if my sister even talked about her will with Alec? Or her prophetic dreams?"

"Guess we'll never know."

On the surface, Mason's words were simple enough, but the finality of that word—*never*—hit Hattie hard. Up until now, she'd been too wrapped up in the ceremony of her sister's death to consider the impact of losing someone she'd dearly loved.

At the hospital, during Melissa's last hours, Hattie had stayed strong for her parents—especially her mom. Then there'd been planning the funeral and reception. Steeling herself for the reading of Melissa's will. Now there was nothing left to do except begin her new life by essentially stepping into her sister's.

How many times when Melissa had been married to Mason had Hattie prayed for just such a thing?

In light of her current situation, this fact shamed her. So much so that the tears she'd so carefully held inside now spilled in ugly sobs.

After handing Vivian to Mason, Hattie dashed upstairs, not even sure where she was going, just knowing she needed to be alone.

Chapter Four

Swell.

Mason glanced over his shoulder at Hattie's departing back, then down at the two sleeping infants. What was he supposed to do now? How had he even landed in this impossible situation?

From somewhere upstairs, a door slammed. But the house wasn't solid enough to mask Hattie's cries.

His heart went out to her. Losing Melissa had to be tough.

He'd have no doubt been upset himself if he hadn't already mourned their relationship's death. Then there was the stunt she'd pulled with her letter—the matchmaking bit. What the hell? Poor Hattie had plenty to be upset about, and he hoped she didn't think he'd taken any of her sister's ramblings seriously.

"Ladies," he mumbled to what amounted to maybe twenty pounds of snoozing babies, "I should probably check on your aunt, but that leaves me in a bind as to what to do with you."

They didn't stir.

Since he already cradled one, he made an awkward position change on the couch in order to scoop up the other. Holding both, he slowly rose, then headed for the kitchen, assuming the kiddy corral would be safe enough until he got back.

Their little arms and legs jolted upon landing.

The house was still on the chilly side, so he left them on their backs, wearing their coats.

At the top of the stairs was a loft library he ventured through to gain access to a hall. He forged down it, intent on not just finding Hattie, but stopping her tears. The sound ripped through him. Took him back to when she'd been thirteen and broke her ankle after using scrap sheet metal for a sled. He'd carried her home and made sure she was okay back then and he'd sure as hell do the same now.

He passed a bedroom, the nursery and a bath before reaching the one closed door Hattie had hidden behind. He opened it to step into what could only be the master. A miniversion of the living room's A-frame window wall overlooked a spectacular snowy night scene.

Hattie sat hunched over and crying on the foot of a king-size bed positioned to take maximum advantage of the view.

Mason's first thought should've been comforting her, but all he seemed able to focus on were Alec and Melissa. What they'd done in that cozy bed. How his wife and best friend had betrayed him to an unimaginable degree.

Snapping himself out of his own issues with the deceased, he sat next to Hattie, easing his arm around her as naturally as he always had. "I'm sorry."

She cried all the harder, struggled to escape him, but he drew her closer, onto his lap, where he held her for all she was worth, all the while gently stroking her hair. "Shh… everything's going to be okay."

"No," she said with a sniffle and shake of her head. "Part of me feels like I did this. I hid so much resentment that she had not one amazing man, b-but two. Then she got the perfect babies I'd always wanted. H-her life was everything mine wasn't. I used to wish I could be her— just for a day. But I never wanted her gone, Mason. I—I loved her so much...."

Sobs racked Hattie's frame, and for the first time since losing Melissa to divorce, Mason felt helpless. As a SEAL, he'd been trained to handle any contingency. Make flash life-or-death decisions, but this one had him stumped. How did he begin comforting Hattie when he harbored such ill will toward her sister and brother-in-law? Now that he was both legally and honor bound to care for their children?

It was too much.

"What if she's somehow looking down on me? And knows I coveted what she had? But I never in a million years wanted it like this. She meant the world to me. More than anything when we were all kids, I wanted to be just like her. As an adult, I realized that wasn't going to happen, but that didn't stop the yearning. Still, I did love her. She has to know. Has to."

"I loved her, too, Hat Trick." He used to call Hattie that when she'd challenged him to pond hockey. "For her to leave you her children, you have to know she loved you every bit as much?"

She nodded.

Drawing back, he lightly touched her chin, urging her to meet his gaze. Though the room was dark, moonlight reflecting off the snow reinforced the fact that she was far from being the little girl and teen Mason remembered. Hattie was all grown up. Even tear-stained, her face was one of the loveliest he'd ever seen. In many ways, she resembled her sister—big brown eyes and long dark hair. Yet she had higher cheekbones, fuller lips. Where she lacked Melissa's petite stature, her full curves made her more womanly.

Pushing back, she turned away, fussing with her hair.

"I'm sorry. I didn't mean to flip out on you like that. Some parent I'll make, huh?"

"Give yourself a break. This is a full-on nightmare—even if neither of us had any issues simmering on the old back burner. Honestly, I didn't even want to come to the funeral and figured the will could be handled via email or over the phone. Dad convinced me I'd regret it if I didn't come."

"Speaking of him, have you let him know?"

Mason shook his head. "I'll give him a call."

A few feet away, she shivered. She crossed her arms and ran her hands up and down them.

He should've gotten off the bed to hold her—at least find a blanket to wrap her in, but his feet were frozen in place.

"Guess I should check on the babies."

"They're fine. As open as this place is, if they were in trouble, we'd hear them crying."

"Still…"

He sighed. "They're *fine*."

Ignoring him, she left the room, heading toward the stairs. A few minutes later, just as he'd suggested, the sound of her cooing over them carried all the way to where he still sat.

Honestly, he felt more than a little shell-shocked by the whole turn of events. Now he was not only mad at Melissa for hooking up with Alec, but for apparently thinking so highly of herself as to presume he'd want her matchmaking services. As if that weren't despicable enough, she'd thought it a good idea to use her own babies as manipulative tools? The whole thing was psycho. He might've long ago loved her, but at the moment, he didn't even kind of like her.

Hattie's big brown eyes flashed before him, reminding

him why he hadn't told Benton to take a flying leap. His being here, in this house, in the very room where Alec and Melissa had made love, wasn't about allegiance to his ex, but her sister.

Hattie had always been there for him and he now owed her the same.

He made a quick call to his dad, bringing him up to speed on the will and how he'd be staying at Melissa and Alec's until his day in court. His dad wasn't the chatty type, so once the facts were delivered, Mason hung up.

Downstairs, he found Hattie removing the girls' coats and soft boots. "Want me to help you get them in their cribs?"

"Sure. But they both need fresh diapers."

He blanched. "Not my idea of a good time, but show me what to do."

Together they took the babies upstairs, and Hattie walked him through a diaper change. "Diaper removal is pretty self-explanatory. From there, use a few wipes, assess if you think she needs rash cream or powder, then—"

"Okay, whoa—I'm great at assessing, but I usually have a list of parameters to work with."

Hattie wrinkled her nose, and damned if she didn't strike him as cute. "You lost me."

"What am I supposed to look for in order to know if either of those contingencies apply?"

She cocked her head. "In English?"

"What am I looking for? Like, if I'm supposed to use the powder or cream, how will I know?"

"Oh. Well, the cream you'll use if anything looks red or irritated. As for the powder…" She shrugged. "Honestly, let's table it for now. I'll look it up online or ask Mom. Pretty sure it's a moisture thing."

"Want me to research it? I'm much better with that than diapering."

"Sure. Thanks." She returned her attention to the baby. "No sign of rash, so we'll grab a fresh diaper, open it, then slide the back part under her—like this."

Stepping alongside her for a better view, he nodded. "Got it. Next?"

"Pull up the front, fasten it with the sticky tabs, put her clothes back on and you're good to go."

"Wait—you didn't say anything about the clothes. All of them come off?"

She sighed. "Now you're being deliberately obtuse."

"No, really. For whatever time I'm here, I want to be as much help as possible. I'm viewing this as a mission."

"Wow. Please tell me you didn't just equate my sister's babies with battle." Keeping one hand on the now-squirmy baby, she grabbed a pair of footie pj's from a nearby drawer.

"What? You don't want my help?"

"Mason, Vanessa and Viv are real-live babies—not burp-and-feed dolls you'd read about in a manual."

"Duh. Why do you think I'm concentrating on what you tell me? I want to get this right. We're in a zero-tolerance mistake zone, right?"

"Wow. Just wow." She finished her task without so much as looking his way.

Whatever. He took her ignoring him as an opportunity to study the nursery layout. Two cribs, built-in shelves loaded with toys and books. Two upholstered swivel rockers. Changing table. Adequate stockpile of supplies on shelf beneath said table. Easy-access traffic flow—although down the line, the potted Norfolk pine in front of the window could pose a spooky shadow problem.

Overall impression? *Way* too much pink.

Once Hattie placed her baby in the crib, Mason took his

turn at diapering. Forcing a deep breath, he rolled down minitights. It was still chilly, so he left the baby's long-sleeved dress, undershirt, sweater and socks on her.

Watching Hattie, the diaper process had seemed straight-forward enough. He easily undid the sticky tape but, upon lifting the front flap, was accosted by a smell so vile he damn near retched.

"Oh, my God..." He stepped back. Fanning the putrid air, he asked, "What the hell? Is she sick?"

Hattie glared. "Welcome to the wonderful world of babies. Lesson 101—poop stinks. Standard operating procedure."

"If that last part was a dig at me, stow it. I'm doing the best I can here, okay?"

Her indifferent shrug told him she wasn't impressed.

Had he really only a few minutes earlier felt sorry for her? Regardless, he forged ahead. "You didn't mention Number Two in your lesson. Any special spray needed? Protective gloves or eyewear?"

"Want me to do it?"

"No." And he was offended she'd asked. "I've got this."

Dear Lord. Mason struggled to maintain his composure while cleaning the baby's behind. Was this poop or tar?

He made the mistake of looking at the kid's face and their gazes connected. Was she smiling? This one had to be Vivian—the baby whose personality matched Melissa's. She'd get a kick out of seeing him tortured.

Finally finished wiping, with Hattie supervising, Mason found a fresh diaper and tried grabbing the kid's ankles to raise her behind, but she kicked so hard it was tough to grab hold. Settling for one ankle, he tried lifting her side-ways, then sneaking the diaper under.

"Not like that," Hattie complained. "You'll put her in traction before her first birthday." Nudging him aside, she dived right in, catching the baby's ankles one-handed on her first try.

"As much as it pains me to admit this," Mason said with a round of applause, "you're good."

"I've had at least a little practice. You'll get the hang of it." She took the diaper from him and, once she had it properly positioned, stepped aside for him to finish. "She's all yours."

When Mason stepped back into place, their arms brushed. The resulting hum of awareness caught him as off guard as practically flunking his first diapering lesson. He and Hattie had never been more than friends, so what was that about? Had she felt it, too? If so, she showed no signs, which told him to chalk it up to his imagination, then get his job done. Another part of him couldn't get Melissa's words from his head. *Hattie has harbored quite the crush on you for as long as she could walk well enough to follow you around.* Could it be true?

Perhaps an even bigger question was, what did he feel for her?

Nothing romantic, that was for sure. For as long as he could remember, she'd been his friend. For sanity's sake, he planned to ignore that rush of attraction in favor of putting Hattie safely back in the friend zone.

Subject closed.

It proved no big deal to get the diaper perfectly positioned, and while a few of his new-father SEAL friends whined about the whole sticky-tab thing being tough to tackle, Mason thought that part a piece of cake. He liked lining them up perfectly straight. Precision in all things—especially diapers—was good.

"There." He couldn't help but smile upon completing his goal. "Now what?"

"Take her dress off and put these on." Hattie offered a pair of pj's that matched Vivian's sister's.

"Just a thought—" Mason struggled to unfasten the row of tiny buttons up the back of the dress "—but what if we started color-coding the twins? That way, we'd know who's who."

"You mean dress Vivian in one color and Vanessa in another?"

"Exactly. That way, they won't be sixteen and realize their whole lives they've been called by the wrong names."

"While I applaud your suggestion, I don't think we're in danger of that. Besides, they already have so many pretty matching clothes, I'd hate to toss everything Melissa bought and was given as shower gifts."

"Hadn't thought of that. When I'm researching powder, I'll see if I can find tips on telling twins apart."

"You do that." Though she didn't smile, he'd have sworn he saw laughter spark her still-teary eyes.

Once both girls had been tucked beneath matching fuzzy pink blankets, Mason asked, "Now what?"

"Know how to do laundry?"

"Sure."

She pointed toward an overflowing hamper. "Mind tackling that while I'm out?"

"Where are you going?"

"I have to at least make an appearance at the bar. I haven't been in since first hearing the news."

"But it's Sunday. Thought no alcohol was sold or served?"

She patted his back. "You *have* been gone awhile. Two years ago, the new mayor, who's a huge Cowboys fan, exempted every Sunday during football season."

As a general rule, Mason never pouted, but he was damn near close. "But I'd rather go with you than be stuck here doing laundry."

"Sorry." She flashed a forced, unapologetic smile. "One of us has to bring home the bacon."

"Hattie Beaumont, you turned mean."

"Nah." She ducked across the hall and into the bathroom. "Just practical."

WITH HER PRACTICAL boots crunching on the city sidewalk's hard-packed snow, Hattie realized she had never been happier to be away from someone in her whole life. Was she really supposed to live with Mason for however long it took him to get unattached from her sister's will? Couldn't he just fly up when it was his turn in court?

Aerosmith's "Walk This Way" spilled out the bar's door at the same time as Harvey Mitchell.

"Got a ride?" Hattie asked.

Breath fogging in the cold night air, he hitched his thumb toward the road. "Wife sent the daughter to pick-me-up." His last three words slurred into one. Looked as though someone should've gone home a few drinks earlier.

Hattie waited outside for the few minutes it took for Harvey's sixteen-year-old, Janine, to show. The bar stood at the end of a pier. She took a deep breath, appreciating the water's briny tang.

With Harvey safely gone, she headed inside, glad for the warmth and cheerful riot of Halloween decorations she'd put up weeks ago before knowing how tragically the month would end.

"Hey, sweetie." Her best friend, Clementine Archer, stepped out from behind the bar, enfolding her in a hug. They'd gone to school together since kindergarten. When Clementine's husband had lost his job at the fish-canning factory, Hattie had suggested her friend take an online bartending class, then come work for her. Five years later, Clementine's husband had run off to Texas, leaving her on her own with their two sons, but she still worked behind the bar four days a week. Her mom watched the boys. "How's it going? You've gotta be a mess."

"Oh—I passed mess a long time ago. I'm currently a disaster." Hattie deposited her purse in a lower cabinet beside the fridge. Before leaving, she needed to run upstairs to switch it out for her usual cargo-style bag. Might as well grab extra clothes, too.

"You leave Mason with the twins?"

Hattie nodded. "He wasn't happy about it. Pouted like a second grader."

"How is it?"

"What?" Hattie poured herself an orange juice on the rocks.

Hands on her hips, Clementine shook her head. "Don't even try playing it cool with me, lady. I'm the one person aside from Melissa who ever knew exactly how much Mason meant to you. No way is his being here not impacting your life."

Hattie looked at her drink. "Yeah, so maybe I'd like a splash of vodka for this, but you know..." She stared at the crowd of regulars: some played pool, others poker, others still watched one of the four flat screens or just talked. Everything about the night was normal, yet not a single thing in Hattie's life felt the same. Her eyes welled with tears again. She blotted them with one of the bar's trademark red plaid napkins she'd had monogrammed with *Hattie's*. "It's all good."

"Oh, sweetie..." Clementine ambushed her with another hug. "You don't still have a thing for him, do you?"

"No. Of course not." Which was why when he'd swooped her into his arms outside of the lawyer's her heart had skipped beats. When he'd stood beside her in her sister's kitchen or they'd shared feeding time on the couch or he'd tugged her onto his lap for a comforting hug, everything she thought she knew turned upside down.

And that was bad.

It didn't matter that Melissa was no longer with them. Mason would always belong to her. Their bond had been unbreakable. So much so that not only had her sister reached from beyond her grave to ask Mason to raise her girls, but she'd had the audacity to suggest he also be Hattie's man.

Chapter Five

"Thanks for bringing all of this by, Dad—and thank you, Fern, for driving." His ditty bag and iPad couldn't be more welcome sights in this unfamiliar home.

While his dad grunted, prune-faced Fern waved off Mason's appreciation in favor of snooping about the kitchen. She'd tossed her red down coat on the granite counter, but still wore her orange cap and a hot-pink sweat suit with striped blue socks. She'd abandoned her sturdy Sorel boots at the front door. "Where'd Melissa keep her coffee?"

"Couldn't tell you."

"Times like these folks need coffee. Hattie didn't make any? And Danish. Doughnuts. At the very least, she could've set out a bag of Oreos."

Mason tried like hell not to smile. "In Hattie's defense, she hardly expected anyone to be here. I'm sure her mother's got plenty of food left from the wake if you two want to head over there?"

"Lord…" Hands on her hips, Fern surveyed Melissa's top-of-the-line Keurig K-Cup–style coffeemaker. "Prissy and downright pretentious is what this is. If I were you, I'd run this straight out to the dump and get you a nice stove-top percolator."

"Sure. I'll see what I can do." What he failed telling

Fern was that he thought the whole single-cup thing pretty damned cool. He'd never known coffee technology existed until his friend Heath's new bride, Patricia, had it listed on her bridal-shower registry. The damn thing had been pricey, so Mason and his pal Cooper had gone halvsies on it. Which reminded him, he needed to call his CO and SEAL team roomie about not being home as scheduled.

"Ready?" His dad, Jerry, joined them. "I've got shows."

Fern furrowed the caterpillars she called brows. "For cryin' out loud, Jer', step into this century. Haven't you heard of a DVR?"

"Haven't you heard the government uses those things to bug your house—they put pinhole spy cams in there, too."

After a grand eye roll, Fern sighed. "S'pose next you'll be telling me sittin' too close to my TV'll make me blind?"

Jerry shrugged. "Judging by your outfit, you may want to push your recliner a ways back."

"Oh, for God's sake…" Mason grabbed Fern's coat and held it out to her. "Get a room and leave me in peace."

"I wouldn't sleep with your father if he laid gold nuggets."

"Thanks for that visual." Wincing, Mason held out the garment, wagging it in hopes of enticing Fern to slip it on and then slip right out the door. "I appreciate you two bringing my gear, but if you don't mind, I've got baby-care research to do. Oh—and, Dad, here are your keys." Mason fished them from his pocket. "Thank you for letting me use your ride."

"No problem, but what're you gonna drive now?"

"I suppose Alec's Hummer."

"Talk about pretentious." Fern snorted. "I don't mean to speak ill of the dead, but I never did approve of that car— if you could even call it that. More like a tank."

Jerry snapped, "You didn't seem to mind much last

winter when you stuck your Shirley Temple curls out the sunroof for the Christmas parade."

"Shut your pie hole, old man. You're just jealous no one asked you."

Fingers to throbbing temples, Mason counted to ten to keep from blowing. Fern and his dad had always been combustible neighbors, but he'd forgotten to what degree. At least they could now retreat to separate vehicles.

After ten more minutes' bickering, Fern and Jerry finally left Mason in peace. Only, even then he didn't truly feel calm because of the emotions warring in his head. Guilt for not feeling more sadness in regard to Melissa's and Alec's deaths, confusion over the sheer logistics of caring for their infant twins, hurt over being treated like a pariah by two families he'd once very much loved and felt a part of.

Thank God for Hattie.

Even though she'd temporarily left him in charge, he appreciated knowing he wasn't ultimately alone. Knowing that by the time the babies woke she'd be back comforted him when otherwise he'd have been in a panic.

Mason tossed a couple logs on the fire, then grabbed his iPad, only to find the battery near dead. He rummaged through his bag for the charger but, when he returned to the sofa to do baby research, found his cord wasn't near long enough.

In need of an extension cord, he headed downstairs to the utility room. His first trek to the home's lowest level, he hadn't ventured farther than the heater. Now he noted the kind of party room he and Alec had only dreamed of when they'd been teens. A fully stocked wet bar complete with two kegs on tap and a loaded wine fridge. A few half-empty beer mugs sat on a counter covered in longneck twist caps sealed in clear acrylic. Mason had never seen anything like it. Had the creation been his idea or Melissa's or their architect or designer's?

A pool table sat lifeless with all the balls scattered as if fresh from a break.

Bright lights from three vintage slots and an assortment of pinball machines and video games stood out in the gloom.

A dozen or so weary red balloons hung at various elevations. Some waist-high. Others an inch from the floor. What had the happy couple been celebrating? Was their current group of friends comprised of the same old crew he'd once also considered his?

He caught a movement in his peripheral vision and discovered Hattie reflected in the mirrored wall behind the bar.

"Impressive, huh?" She trailed her fingertips along a felt-covered poker table still littered with cards and chips. "Almost as nice as my bar on the wharf, but I have more than one TV." Gesturing to a wall-mount model that was damn near half the size of his truck, she swiped at glistening tears. Her faint smile twisted his heart. He couldn't imagine what she must be going through.

"If you don't mind my asking…" He swatted a balloon. "What were they celebrating?"

"Remember Craig Lovett from your senior class?"

He nodded.

"It was his birthday." Behind the bar, she took the three mugs and washed them in the sink. "I'm surprised Melissa left even this little of a mess. Practically her only hobby was cleaning."

"Fun." He snagged the nearest balloon. "Want me to grab all of these?"

"Sure. Thanks." Though it'd been years since their last meaningful conversation, Hattie's current cool demeanor unnerved him. A childish part of him wanted things back the way they used to be between them. Hattie had been his go-to girl for when he'd just wanted to chill. They'd always been able to talk about anything from sports to politics to, hell, even stupid issues like annoying road construction.

Now he wasn't sure what to say.

Her new, more polished, infinitely more curvy look threw him for a loop. Not only didn't she look the same, but she carried herself with more confidence. Shoulders back, long hair loose, wind-tossed to the point of being a little wild. Her scent even threw him. Gone was the tomboy blend of sweat and bubble gum, replaced by a complex crispness that on this snowy night embodied the town's conifer trees and ice.

"Here's a trash bag." She held the top open for him while he shoved in the balloons. She was quiet for a moment and then said, "What's wrong?"

"Not sure what you mean?" He focused on his task rather than her uncomfortable proximity.

"You're tensed up—kind of like when we were in grade school and all of you guys used to freeze when the girls threatened to give you cooties."

"Whatever…" He shook his head. "I'm just tired." Of the whole situation. If Melissa and Alec hadn't died, he'd be safe and sound back in Virginia—even better, off on a mission where his thoughts were occupied 24/7 by things that mattered. The issues currently fogging his brain were the kinds of details he found best avoided. Women and kids were so far off his radar they might as well be alien life forms.

"Me, too. Hopefully, after a good night's rest all of this will feel less overwhelming." Her eyes shone.

Mason knew he should say something kind and reassuring, but how could he when panic consumed him? Even worse, once they met with the judge, his ties to the whole mess would be cut, but poor Hattie was stuck with two kids for a lifetime. Inconceivable. "Yeah. I bet everything will seem better in the morning."

HATTIE WOKE TO the not-so-melodic sound of her nieces screaming. She bolted from her guest-room bed, nearly colliding with Mason as he charged up the stairs from where he'd slept on the sofa.

She winced. "Thought you said everything would be better in the morning?"

"Yeah, well, guess I was wrong. You take the one on the left. I'll take the right."

Hattie scooped squalling Vivian from her crib.

Mason picked up Vanessa.

Neither baby showed any sign of calming soon. Above her nieces' now-frantic tears, Hattie shouted, "I'm guessing both need fresh diapers and feeding, so should we divide and conquer?"

"What do you mean?" He lightly jiggled Vanessa, which only agitated her further.

"I'll make bottles while you handle morning cleanup." Honestly, could her sister have left her in any worse position? The instant upgrade from aunt to mom was rough enough; tossing in an incompetent baby daddy like Mason compounded her already-considerable woes.

His eyebrows shot up. "You mean you're leaving me alone with them?"

After placing Vivian temporarily back in her crib, she patted Mason's back. "I have total faith in you to do a great job."

Five minutes later, bottles in hand, she'd just mounted the steps to check on Mason's progress when she spied him carrying both babies and heading her way. Vivian and

Vanessa were still red-eyed and huffing, but at least the near-deafening wails had calmed. While moments earlier, she'd have seen this as a good thing, the lull in the storm afforded her the relative luxury of getting her first good look at Mason that morning. He wore no shirt and a pair of low-riding sweats with *Navy* written down one leg. He'd always had a great body, but now? Wow.

Mouth dry, she hastily looked away from six-pack abs partially blocked by her squirmy nieces.

She met him halfway up the stairs, taking Vanessa. "Did you have any trouble?"

"Nah. Compared to bomb demo, diapering's no biggie. This one's a pistol, though. Fights me every step of the way." Taking the bottle she offered, he nodded to Vivian. "She's only four arms and legs shy of being a human octopus. I feel bad for you when she learns to walk."

Hattie laughed, though inside, his innocent statement brought on cause to worry. The twins still had months before they started walking, but the day would come. She'd soon need to worry about baby-proofing and figuring out solid foods and brushing tiny teeth. She didn't even want to think about the girls walking yet.

She settled onto the sofa with her charge.

Mason, cradling Vivian, sat on the opposite end. He initially fumbled getting the bottle into the baby's crying mouth, but once he did, the house fell blessedly quiet. "That's better. When they tag team like that, I feel desperate."

"Me, too...."

After a few minutes' companionable silence, he asked, "What's the plan for today?"

"I suppose we need to nail down a firm date for you to appear in court. Then, if you don't mind, I could use help moving a few things from my place over here."

"Sure." He repositioned Vivian. "Think your mom would feel up to watching these two?"

"I don't see why not."

"Good." His smile did funny things to her stomach. "I don't know about you, but I could use a breather."

"We've only been awake ten minutes."

He shrugged. "There's no politically correct way for me to say this, so I'll just go for it. Have you thought about taking the same route I am? You know, signing over your parental rights?"

"You mean passing the buck?"

His smile morphed into a scowl. "I mean, getting your life back on track. Your mom seemed genuinely upset that she won't be raising these two. Why not give her what she wants? Hell, give a girl to Alec's mom, too. That way, they can each have a kid, all problems solved."

"Hear that rushing sound? That was my respect for you, flying out the window."

"How LONG ARE you going to stay mad at me?" Mason asked Hattie as they snatched boxes from her dad's warehouse's recycling bin.

"Forever." She wouldn't even look his way.

They'd each spelled each other for showers, then loaded the eight tons of gear needed to drop the babies with Akna. During all that time, she'd barely said three words.

When Benton had called, dropping the bomb that it would be three weeks before Mason's meeting with the Valdez judge, the mood hadn't grown much brighter.

"Look," Mason said, "I was only stating the obvious. What you're doing for Melissa is a noble, lovely gesture, but it's also going way above and beyond when if you get right down to it, what did your sister ever do for you? Melissa was a taker. She took from me and you."

"Stop." Tears shone on Hattie's cheeks, making Mason instantly ashamed, even though in his heart he believed he'd spoken the truth. "What happened to you? I never remember you being this cruel."

"Cruel?" He couldn't contain a sarcastic laugh. "Is there a statute of limitations on me being allowed to harbor ill will toward a woman who essentially ruined my life?"

"Stop being a drama queen. That all happened years ago."

"Right—" he grabbed an undamaged box and tossed it on their pile "—just like the time Melissa totaled her car and instead of making her earn a new one, your parents gave her yours? Or how about when you won the role of Juliet in the school play, but then Melissa told the drama teacher she should get it since I was playing Romeo and we were dating, and that would sell more tickets?"

Hattie sharply looked away. "I refuse to do this. Melissa's dead. Whatever she did back then is ancient history. Right now, her babies need a mom—they already have grandmothers. My mother and Alec's mean well, but you, of all people, should realize what it's like growing up without a mom."

"Leave my past out of this." Jaw clenched, he pitched a box hard enough at their growing pile to crush one of the corners.

"But it's all right for you to air my dirty laundry?"

"I gave you Melissa-specific examples."

"I'm done with this discussion." She raised her chin. The air outside the loading dock was cold enough to see her sharp exhalations manifest in angry clouds. Her cheeks reddened, probably more from fury than cold. Regardless, her determined stare reminded him of better days. Times when that determination landed them on epic climbs to mountaintops and fishing in places he'd sworn they'd never find their way home from. She'd been one of his best pals, but for whatever reason, that dynamic had changed, which made him sad. He'd already lost her sister; he didn't want to lose Hattie's friendship, as well.

"I'm sorry," he said. "I can see where my suggestion could come across as crass, but, Hat Trick, you're no more ready to be a parent than I am. I was only trying to give you an *out*."

"That's just it…" She brushed away more tears. "I don't want an out. These are my nieces we're talking about— not a pair of Yorkies. If Melissa had enough faith in me to handle the job, then I can. Period."

"Okay. I get it." Had she always been this beautiful? Her anger intensified the color in her high cheekbones, making her appear warrior-fierce. In that moment, he believed she could single-handedly raise the twins. He just wished she didn't have to. But did he wish it enough to quit the navy? Stay in Conifer to help?

Not just *no. Hell no.*

Chapter Six

"Clem, come on—focus." Hattie waved her hand in front of her friend's blatant stare. "Can you cover for me tonight?"

"I remember Mason being decent looking, but *damn*..."

"Hush." Hattie gave her friend a well-placed elbow to her side as Mason effortlessly hefted another box down the narrow staircase that led from her apartment to the bar's main floor. "He's nothing special."

"Says the girl who lusted after him for the vast majority of her life—at least until her sister married him."

"Can you please save this for another time?" Hattie closed her eyes on the not-too-shabby view of Mason's jean-clad behind.

"Look, I understand what you're going through must be rough, but Melissa dumped him a long time ago. In my mind, that makes him fair game."

"Please stop."

"He's single. You're single. Those babies go to bed early, leaving a whole lot of time for fooling—"

"Hush!" Hattie hadn't meant to shout, but when the five patrons at the bar looked her way, she reddened. Her voice at a more appropriate level, she said, "You're being ridiculous. Now back to the topic at hand—can you cover for me tonight, or not?"

"Sorry, but Dougie's got a nasty cold. Once I'm done

here, I wanna run him over to the urgent-care clinic to get him checked out."

"How's Joey?" Clementine's son Doug was three and Joey was five.

"So far, he's fine. But Mom had sniffles when I dropped Dougie off this morning. If she goes down, I'm screwed."

"Hopefully, they'll both feel better soon." Hattie had five other bartenders she could call, but she thought working the shift herself, and having a night away from Mason, would probably do her good.

He appeared. "That was the last of it. Ready to head out?"

"Sure." Hattie took her purse from behind the bar. "But I'll need to come back later."

He frowned. "Clem, how've you been?"

"Good, thanks." Oh, for heaven's sake. Clementine visibly flushed. Mason wasn't *that* great to look at.

The lie created heat in her own cheeks. Okay, so Mason wasn't exactly unfortunate when it came to his appearance, but that didn't mean Clementine's matchmaking had been warranted. The whole issue was wildly inappropriate.

"Hear you've done real good for yourself." Hattie's friend actually fluffed her hair. "Even so, we've missed you around here."

"Thanks." He shrugged. "It's nice being back. Just wish the circumstances were better."

"I understand." Could Clementine be more obvious? She'd struck a pose against the bar that showed a royal gorge of cleavage. "We're all pretty upset."

Really, Clem? The only thing she looked upset about was Mason standing too far away.

"Okay, well…" Hattie grabbed Mason by his arm, tugging him toward the door. "Glad you two could catch up, but I'd like to unpack all my stuff at Melissa's before it's time to pick up the girls."

Outside, though the day was sunny, a blustery north wind seized Hattie's hair, tangling it in her face.

"Hold up." Mason stopped her midway down the pier, way too deep into her personal space for her liking while helping her tidy the mess. "You look like Cousin Itt from— What was that show?"

"The Addams Family?" For years, they'd watched the show every day after school. Hattie could probably still recite every episode.

"Yeah. That's it." Resuming their walk, he said, "I used to love that show."

"Me, too." Only not for the stellar acting, but because Melissa had hated it, which meant Hattie and Mason were usually left alone with the TV and Oreos.

At her SUV, he asked, "Want me to drive?"

"Why?"

"You look tired. And a couple times when you were packing, I caught you crying."

She yanked open the driver's-side door with extra force, then climbed behind the wheel. "I'm fine. In fact, having just lost my sister, I figure I'm doing pretty damned good to even be upright."

"Excellent point," he said from beside her. "You are putting on a good show of strength, Hat Trick, but I know you. It's a show. Honestly, you look ready to break."

"Thanks for the appraisal, but you *used* to know me." She started the car and pulled away from the curb. "Now? I'm not sure what we are. Maybe strangers who used to be friends?"

HATTIE'S ASSESSMENT OF their relationship sobered Mason. While she unpacked her belongings in the guest bedroom, he lounged on the living room sofa, surfing the web for baby-care sites. He was determined to treat this bump in his road as he would any other mission. Professionally, with a cool detachment from any issue close to getting personal.

They were due at Hattie's mom's in a couple hours, so he made good use of the uninterrupted time.

He'd just found an excellent page outlining the reasons for not using baby powder when a crash sounded from upstairs, followed by a feminine yelp.

"Hattie? You okay?"

When she didn't answer, he abandoned his iPad to charge up the stairs.

He found her beneath a pile of clothes tall enough to have damn near buried her. Looked as if the closet's hanging rod had given up the ghost. "Damn, girl, good thing you use plastic hangers or you'd have poked out your eyes."

She popped her head out from between the legs of faded jeans. "Less commentary and more help would be appreciated."

"Oh, I don't know…" He couldn't resist tugging his phone from his back pocket to snap a quick pic. The closet was a walk-in, but Hattie and her sweaters, jeans and blouses occupied a huge portion of the floor. "I think we should sit back for a minute to savor the moment."

"You're a beast." She gave a mighty shove to the clothes in front of her, struggling to get back on her feet.

"A good-looking one, though," he teased, offering her his hands to tug her free from the mess.

Her only answer was a glare.

"How'd you manage this? I always thought Melissa was the fashionista?"

"Have you seen the size of her closet? Trust me, this

isn't much. I guess she and Alec just used cheap rod brackets when this place was built."

"In their defense—" Mason grabbed as much clothing as he could, piling it on the bed "—probably most guests don't have as much stuff as you."

For a brief moment, the old Hattie stuck out her tongue. It happened so fast, Mason couldn't even be sure he hadn't imagined her return to that old playful habit, but he hoped he hadn't. Holding her hands even for the brief seconds it'd taken to free her from the fabric avalanche hadn't felt ordinary, but somehow special. As if he'd stumbled across a long-forgotten part of himself that up until now, he hadn't even known was missing.

He looked at Hattie.

Really looked, and found himself riveted by the view. Even with her long hair more disheveled than usual and her cheeks prettily flushed, there was something about her that kept drawing him in. The fact that she wore the hell out of faded jeans and a plaid shirt didn't hurt, either. The woman had curves in all the right places.

Hands on her hips, she asked, "What?"

"Huh?"

"You're staring." She fussed with her hair. "Do I have a bra hanging from my head?"

He laughed. "Can't a guy appreciate a nice view?"

EVEN AT TEN that night while working her shift at the bar, Hattie struggled to get Mason's cryptic words from her head. When he'd mentioned that "nice view," she'd been standing in front of French doors that led to a balcony overlooking the valley. At that moment, she'd brushed off his unexpected comment, but now her stomach knotted. Had he been talking about her?

No. She scrubbed harder at the greasy hot-wing residue someone had smeared on the bar. For as long as they'd known each other, Melissa had been the only girl for him. Their divorce, and even her death, couldn't erase that kind of history.

Mason had 100 percent admired scenic Treehorn Valley. Which was a good thing. According to unwritten, yet explicitly understood Sister Code, Mason would always belong to Melissa. As he should. Even if he did by some miracle find her attractive, Hattie had more pride than to even want a man who no doubt viewed her as second best.

"Didn't expect to find you here." A familiar voice jolted Hattie from her thoughts.

"I could say the same to you." She jogged around to the bar's front to hug her dad. With dark circles under his tear-reddened eyes, he was a walking example of how shattered their whole family felt. "Why aren't you with Mom?"

Shifting on his stool, resting his elbows on the bar, he sighed. "She hasn't had a decent night's rest since…" In that small hesitation, Hattie all-too-easily filled in the blank. "I called Doc Amesbury to prescribe her a sedative. She's finally asleep."

"What about you? Not that I'm knocking the healing benefits of the occasional shot of whiskey, but, Dad, maybe you should've also gotten medicine for yourself?"

He waved off her concern. "I might look like hell, but I'm all right. Need to stay strong for your mom. She's already torn up enough about your sister, but to then have the twins taken from her, too…" He shook his head. "I get what your sister was trying to accomplish, but in the process she broke your mother's heart."

Hattie struggled to compose her thoughts. "Are you suggesting I follow Mason's lead and sign away my rights?"

"No. Absolutely not—unless you want to. Your mom likes to believe she can do anything and everything, but as exhausted as she was from watching the rug rats this afternoon, no way is she ready to start parenting all over again from scratch."

On autopilot, Hattie poured her dad two fingers of his favorite bourbon.

"I think what she doesn't realize, but your sister in some crazy way did, is that if your mom were to assume primary custody of those babies, she'd for all practical purposes lose out on the joy she finds in being their grandmother." He took a long sip of his drink. "You and I were blessed to have both in our lives, and there's a difference."

Hattie nodded. Though all of her grandparents had passed—her maternal grandmother just two years earlier— Hattie would never forget the unconditional love and down- right spoiling she'd found in their loving arms.

"That said, if you feel like you can't handle raising those girls on your own, move home. Between the three of us, we'll figure it out."

"Dad, I'm fine." And one of these days, possibly years down the road, she'd believe it. For now, all she could do was honor her sister's last wish as best she could. "I'm sorry Mom's upset. She's not mad at me, is she?"

He shook his head. "More like mad at the world." After another drink, he said, "Give it some time. I'm sure she'll come around."

HATTIE DIDN'T CLOSE until 2:00 a.m., meaning by the time she'd poured her last customer into the town's only cab, it was two-thirty when she reached Melissa and Alec's.

Would the supersize house ever feel like home?

The night had turned bitterly cold and her footfalls crunched in the icy snow.

By the time true winter cold set in, she'd have to sell her ancient SUV in favor of driving Melissa's much-newer

Land Rover that was parked all warm and toasty in the garage.

She'd just mounted the freshly shoveled porch when the door opened and Mason stepped out.

"Hey." He held the door open for her.

"Hey, yourself. Why are you still up?" Brushing past him, Hattie found herself wrapped in his all-masculine scent of sweet woodsmoke and the leathery aftershave he'd started using in tenth grade. She wanted to act as if it was no big deal, but at this time of night her defenses were down and the comfort of their shared pasts stirred a warmth she'd thought gone forever.

He shrugged. "Couldn't sleep till I knew you'd made it home safe."

"Thanks."

With her inside, he closed and locked the door—not that there was much need for it with Conifer's almost-nonexistent crime rate.

"Hungry?" He took her coat and hung it in the entry-hall closet. "I made a couple boxes of mac and cheese."

"Yum," she teased. "Didn't know you'd become a gourmet."

"If that was a dig at me flunking home ec, I shouldn't have even been in there and you know it." Only in Alaska could the woodshop teacher be on extended leave because of a bear attack. "If I'd had a little longer, that cake would've been delicious."

"Yeah, yeah…" She couldn't help but grin at his dear face that had changed so much over the years, but in her mind's eye not at all. "Keep telling yourself that. One of these days it might come true."

"Just for that, next time you're at work, I'm making you a cake so you'll be forced to eat your words." While she removed her boots, he took a covered bowl from the fridge.

"From scratch?"

He put the bowl in the microwave. "Is there any other kind?"

"Sure. Duncan Hines, Pillsbury and the really fancy ones from Ann's Bakery."

Leaning against the counter, waiting for the food to warm, he grinned. "How is it that after all these years, you're still a pain in my ass?"

"Language," she said primly. "You forget, children are present."

"Whatever." The microwave dinged.

Hattie sat at the counter bar while Mason delivered her a fork and the bowl of leftovers. What the meal lacked in flavor, it made up for in companionship. She'd forgotten how much fun she and Mason could have with simple banter.

He took a beer from the fridge and twisted off the cap. After hefting himself up to sit on the kitchen's island counter, he asked, "In all seriousness, how are you?"

"I'm good. Don't get me wrong, this isn't going to be an easy adjustment, but I'll deal. What about you? You're the one who pulled the short end of the straw tonight. How were my adorable nieces?"

His handsome half smile did funny things to Hattie's insides. "Vanessa was a doll, but I swear Vivian's got it in for me. During bath time, she pitched soap in my eyes and I'm pretty sure she deliberately tried to drown my cell."

"Uh-huh…" Now Hattie was the one grinning. "All this from an infant who can barely roll herself over?"

"Don't let that innocent act fool you." He raised his bottle. "She's a tough cookie. Before too long, you'll be catching her smoking out behind the woodshed."

"Right. If my memory serves me correct, that was you and Melissa who got caught in that particular act."

"There was never any proof we smoked those butts.

Could've been anyone." He winked before hopping down to finish off his beer and toss the bottle in the recycling bin. "Ready for bed?"

"I should be—" she speared a few noodles "—but I'm too wired. Wanna watch a movie—or at least part of one?"

He yawned. "Sounds better than another night on the sofa."

"There is another bed."

A scowl marred his otherwise-gorgeous face. "Yeah, and it's got more ghosts than the town graveyard."

MASON WOKE GOD-ONLY-KNEW how many hours later in the basement's home theater to the sound of the opening loop for *Alien* playing over and over. Laced in with that were frantic cries from upstairs.

A glance to his left showed Hattie out cold, lightly snoring.

Bolting to action, Mason raced from the room to find bright sun streaming through the living room's glass wall. The baby monitor he'd meant to carry downstairs with them sat on the kitchen counter, echoing the twins' wails.

Feeling lower than low—like the worst babysitter in the history of the world, Mason bounded up the stairs and into the nursery. "I'm so sorry, ladies."

He scooped first Vanessa, then Vivian into his arms. Vanessa calmed soon enough, letting out offended huffs, but there was no consoling Vivian.

After making a precision-swift diaper change, Mason marched downstairs with his troops, setting them in the playpen while mixing formula. A few minutes after that, he sat on the sofa with both pretty girls nestled into the crooks of his arms.

"I'm so sorry," he said over their greedy suckling. "Rookie mistake that will *never* happen again."

Vivian's blue-eyed stare warned him it'd better not.

The fact that he'd forgotten such a basic necessity as the baby monitor reinforced Mason's belief he had no business being any child's parent—let alone, Melissa and Alec's kids.

Though Hattie claimed she was ready, he had serious doubts as to whether or not she was any more capable than him. Not three minutes into the movie, clearly exhausted, she'd fallen asleep.

He'd watched her for a spell, worrying about how she'd manage both her bar and new family.

She'd always been one of the strongest people he knew, but in that moment's peace, she'd appeared vulnerable. Almost fragile. Her complexion had paled and her cheeks bore telltale signs of tears.

Guilt consumed him for even thinking of leaving her on her own with the girls. But honestly, what else could he do? Even if the twins weren't the product of a marriage he'd viewed as a betrayal, that whole mess had forever changed him. It'd stolen whatever softness his heart might have once contained and exchanged it for unyielding steel.

He was now a soldier.

That was all.

Chapter Seven

"I'm a horrible person," Hattie said as she pushed their cart at Conifer's only grocery store. While Princess Vivian rode in her carrier in the cart, Mason held Vanessa. "You should've shaken me awake."

"Knock it off, will you?" He took five cans of the organic formula Melissa had preferred from the shelf. "We both screwed up. I'm as much to blame as you. Luckily, other than Vivian giving me the stink eye, no real harm was done."

She tossed three bags of diapers atop their growing pile. "Yeah, but what if there'd been a fire or burglar?"

"Armed robbery a big worry in Conifer nowadays?"

It took Hattie a sec to see the smile lighting his eyes. Then she restrained herself from pummeling him. "You know what I mean."

"Yeah, I do. But we got lucky and both girls are fine. Lesson learned." They rounded the corner to the cereal aisle, where he asked, "You still a fan of Cap'n Crunch?"

"Love it," she said with a wistful glance toward a box, "but my hips don't."

"What's wrong with your hips?"

Seriously? He was going to make her explain the obvious? She'd always been big-boned, but lately her weight had become more and more of an issue. One she had no intention of discussing with Mason.

"Did you have an operation Dad forgot to tell me about?"

Hattie clenched her teeth to keep from saying something she may later regret. After adding bran flakes to the cart, she asked, "Anything in particular you want?"

"Whoa." She'd moved a good ten feet from him, when he grabbed her arm, lightly tugging her back, flooding her with an old, achy longing for him she'd thought had been tucked safely away and forgotten. "Talk to me, Hat Trick. What's with the sudden deep freeze?"

Tears stung her eyes. Her friends constantly told her how strong she was and funny and hardworking, but never had anyone said she was pretty or looked darling in a dress the way they had her sister. She would give away half her credit score to have Mason look at her just once the way he had Melissa. With heat. Longing. Appreciation.

"What'd I do? Does this have something to do with missing your sister?"

Wrenching free from him, she continued to the next aisle, desperate to get away.

Unfortunately, he was not only a head taller than her, but faster. In a heartbeat, he'd rounded the cart, bracing his hands on either side. "You're not going anywhere until I'm out of the doghouse. If we're stuck living together for the next three weeks, let's at least be civil."

Stuck? Oh—that made her feel much better.

"For the last time, what do your hips have to do with our old pal The Captain?"

"I'm fat, okay? There. I said it. Happy?"

He actually had the good graces to appear dumbfounded, with his mouth partially open. "Are you kidding me?"

"Can we please finish up?" Unshed tears blurred her vision.

"We will, but first things first. For the record, what the hell? Fat? You're not fat, for God's sake. You're voluptuous and a one-hundred-percent beautiful woman. Melissa used to spout this dieting crap all the time and it pissed me off. If I were sticking around, I'd tell Vanessa and Viv every day that they're pretty just the way they are."

But you're not sticking around. The words caught in Hattie's throat. For an awkward moment, she wasn't sure what to do with herself and then Mason caught and held her gaze.

Finally, he looked away before stalking to the delicious, sugary cereal they'd both eaten by the bushels as kids. He tossed two boxes in the cart, then shot her a dirty look. "You're not fat."

"WOULD YOU QUIT lookin' at that thing and get back to chopping?" Mason's dad rammed his ax extra hard on the log he'd been splitting, coming dangerously close in the process to knocking off the baby monitor Mason had set on the porch rail. The temperature was falling fast, and a stiff breeze howled through the pines. With another winter storm heading their way, and Alec not even having a fraction of the wood supply needed to carry a home as large as his and Melissa's through the winter, Mason was grateful to his dad for pitching in. "Fern knows more about babies than anyone in this town."

"How?" Hattie had gone to work at the bar and her father reported Akna was in no shape to watch the girls, so Fern, a former long-haul trucker, had volunteered to watch Vivian and Vanessa.

"Remember a few years back when Fern had that puppy? Well, Rascal grew into a fine dog."

"Dad, even I know there's a helluva difference between raising a dog and kids."

His father used his shirt sleeve to wipe sweat from his brow. "Fern's a good woman. Those kids could do worse."

"Since when are you two getting on so well?"

"What do you mean?" Had his longtime bachelor dad's cheeks actually reddened from something other than exertion?

"You know…" Mason winked. "I think Fern has a crush on you."

"Me and Fern?" Jerry laughed. "We have a complicated relationship. Although, folks at the coffee shop have been speculating on the prospect of you and Hattie ending up together. Said it'd be shameful—Hattie taking up with her dead sister's husband."

"They can talk all they want—" Mason took a fresh log from the truck bed "—but not only did the gossips leave out the bit about Melissa's having been my ex, but I'm expected back on base in three weeks. Besides which, one Beaumont woman was more than enough for me."

His dad grunted. "Guess you've got a point there."

"You're actually agreeing with me?"

"Not so much agreeing as remembering. Not to speak ill of the dead, but Melissa put you through the ringer. Alec, too. Wasn't right. Still…" He stopped chopping to lean back against their growing, neatly stacked pile. "I suppose if I'm ever going to get grandkids, sooner or later you're gonna have to climb back on that horse."

Mason winced. "If only it were that simple. And since when did you start wanting to be a grandpa?"

"I'm getting up in years. For that matter, so are you." He resumed chopping. "Speaking from past experience, growing old alone isn't all it's cracked up to be."

"Then why don't you find a good woman? And when you do, then you can leave me alone."

"Jerry, hon?" Fern poked her head out the front door. "You two want chili or tacos for dinner?"

"Hon?" Mason aimed a smile in his dad's direction. "If I were you, I'd take that as a sign." As for his own love life? Those days were long gone.

"WHAT'S WRONG WITH HER?" Hattie asked her dad, who was sorting his DVD collection. When he'd reported earlier that her mom was too sick to watch the twins, Hattie worried the rest of the day.

"Not sure."

She removed her coat and boots to curl onto an end of the sofa. Strange how the room looked the same as it always had. Soothing blue walls covered in dozens of family pictures. Hand-crocheted doilies covering tabletops decorated with lamps and her mom's many ballerina figurines. A stranger looking in would never suspect the tragedy their family was going through. "What are Mom's symptoms?"

Rather than look at her, he studied the back cover of a DVD case. "Pretty sure she's just tired."

"But she loves caring for the girls." Standing, she said, "I'll talk to her."

"Wish you wouldn't." Her dad abandoned his movie to block the hall.

"Okay, now you're scaring me. What's going on?"

"She's having a hard time with this—we both are."

"By 'this,' do you mean what happened to Melissa? Or are you talking about the will?"

After a sharp exhalation, he shook his head. "Leave it alone."

"Okay. Sure." Hattie had tired of crying, but the knot

that had become all too familiar at the back of her throat made it difficult to breathe.

Though the last thing she wanted was to be distanced from her parents when she needed them most, Hattie abided by her father's wishes and left the two of them alone.

"It was awfully nice of Fern and your dad to step in to help." Hattie passed Mason the last of the plates to dry.

Vivian and Vanessa shared the playpen, alternating between gumming teething rings and each other. It was good for a change, seeing them not upset.

"With Fern watching the girls, Dad and I got a lot of wood cut."

"Thanks." The pain of her father's rejection still stung, and though Hattie had held her emotions in check while sharing their meal with Jerry and Fern, she now felt dangerously near her breaking point. Not a good thing considering the meltdown she'd already had that morning at the grocery store. "I really appreciate your help. While you're still in town, I need to get a new schedule established at the bar."

"Sure. I'm happy to do whatever you need."

Though his words were kind, as were his actions, Hattie couldn't help feeling tension simmering between them. Despite the years between them, she still felt as if she knew him better than just about anyone—at least anyone other than Melissa. His shoulders were too squared for him to be relaxed. The set of his jaw too tight.

They finished washing and drying the dishes. While Hattie wiped down the counters, Mason brushed crumbs from the place mats Fern had set on the table.

"Look," Hattie finally said, unable to bear a moment's more tension, "about this morning at the store... I was—"

"Stop. I should've stayed out of your business." He left the table, approaching her until he stood perilously close. "But I meant it, you know? Hat Trick, you're a beautiful woman. One day, you're going to make some lucky guy seriously happy."

But not you?

After what she'd just been through with her dad, the last thing Hattie needed was Mason's vacuous compliment. What he didn't know—what he must never know—was that no matter how many guys she'd dated, none of them had ever meant more to her than him. Melissa had known it. Hattie was still furious with her for matchmaking via her will. That letter should've been a treasured keepsake, but instead, Hattie found her sister's last words mortifying. Before losing her sister, Hattie's life's tragedy had been loving a man she could never have. It struck her as ironic that even with Melissa no longer in the picture, Mason was just as off-limits—not only because of her own conscience, but his clichéd "some lucky guy" declaration.

Covering her face with her hands, she wasn't sure how much more she could take.

"Hattie?" With his elbow, he delivered what she assumed he meant to be a playful nudge. The kind of gesture he'd made a hundred times when they'd been friends and later, when by law he'd technically been her brother. "I know this pouty look. What's going on? With Fern and my dad here, I didn't have the chance to ask if everything's okay with your mom."

She pitched the dishrag in the sink. "No. Things are far from okay with both of my folks. Though Dad wouldn't give me specifics, I'm guessing Mom's still freaking out about the will."

"I'm sorry." He drew her into a hug. The kind of friendly gesture they'd exchanged countless times.

His strength, his warmth, his mere presence meant more to her than he would ever know. She had to pull herself together. Grief was making her an emotional basket case when she'd always prided herself on being strong.

"A few months from now, when you're settled into your new routine, I'll bet things will be better."

"Hope you're right." Hattie pressed her cheek against his impossibly toned chest. Her mother's words had been so cruel, yet in the same respect, given the opportunity, would she not only kiss Mason, but more?

For the longest time, they stood together, bodies so close they'd become one. She allowed herself the weakness of letting him be the strong one, because she was tired of holding it all together when all she wanted was to fall apart.

She glanced up at him, at his dear lips. How long had she dreamed of holding him like this? Having him hold her? Hattie had been mortified by Melissa spilling Hattie's most closely guarded secret about her crush on Mason. How embarrassing, but at the same time, liberating. For if all of her cards were already on the table, what did she have to lose by standing on her tiptoes, touching her lips to his for so brief a tantalizing second? She wasn't sure she had actually kissed him at all. But then he groaned, easing his hand under the curtain of her hair, and suddenly what she'd meant to be a simple gesture turned very complicated, and he was kissing her, sweeping her tongue, chilling her yet warming her, until everything in the room vanished, save for him and the raw emotions their connection evoked.

"Oh, my God..." Just as shockingly as the kiss had begun, it ended. "I'm sorry. That shouldn't have happened."

"No, *I'm* sorry...." Her hands pressed to her swollen, still-tingling lips. *Mortification* didn't come close to describing how deeply she regretted what had just transpired. "It'll never happen again."

"Of course. Shouldn't have happened the first time."

"Agreed."

For an endless minute, they stood frozen. Just as well, considering Hattie didn't have a clue where to go from here. She'd kissed her dead sister's ex-husband. On the morality meter, she couldn't get much lower.

"On a lighter note…" Mason rocketed to the other side of the kitchen. "Did you know that at six months, a baby's brain will have already grown to half the size of an adult's?"

In no mood for baby trivia, Hattie simply stared.

"YOU LOOK LIKE death warmed over."

"Love you, too," Hattie said to Clementine early the next evening upon arriving to tend bar for the rest of the night.

"Sorry, but are you getting enough sleep?"

Hattie's only reply was a sad laugh.

"Wait—let me guess. Mason's not helping out with the babies?"

"Guess again. Turns out he's SEAL Nanny. When the twins are sleeping, he researches infant care online, then somehow assimilates it, only to brag about all he knows, which leads to making me feel guilty for all I don't know."

"Chin up." Clementine took her purse from under the counter. "In a few weeks, Mason will be gone, and with any luck, you won't have to deal with him again."

"Guess you're right." What Hattie couldn't share with her friend was that she feared Mason's leaving was a big part of her problem. He'd already adopted the role of the twins' primary caregiver. He could practically change a diaper one-handed and somehow managed feeding both girls their bottles at the same time. The guy was like a highly trained human octopus!

Clementine took her gloves from her purse. "I'm having a Halloween party next Saturday night. You and Mason wanna come?"

"Thanks, but I'm sure Mason would feel awkward around the old crowd and my mom's acting weird, so I don't know if she'd watch the twins. Plus, I really should be here. On any holiday, you know how it's usually nuts."

"Which is why Trevor and Rose have volunteered to cover for you. Come on—" she gave Hattie an elbow nudge "—say yes. It'll be fun."

"I'll think about it."

"You have to at least take the babies to Wharf-o-Ween." Hattie had forgotten about the town's annual Halloween festival that was held on the wharf –hence the kooky name.

Hattie sighed. "I don't know. We'd have to get costumes, and what if people talked? You know—like it's too soon after losing Melissa to have her kids out partying?"

"So what if they do? Melissa might be gone, but the whole reason she left her girls with you is for them to live. Meaning the question you have to ask yourself is, what would she want you to do?"

A WEEK PASSED.

Mason wished he could shake the melancholy that had settled over Hattie, but they seemed to have fallen into a rhythm of orchestrated avoidance—at least on Hattie's part.

Whenever he tried talking with her about anything more in depth than weather, she dashed off to her room—which made him crazy because he really needed to debrief. Compared to his usual workdays, caring for the twins was no big deal physically. What got to him was the mental game of sitting by himself all day every day. Sure, his dad and Fern dropped in occasionally, but other than them, he'd been pretty much left on his own.

Which was making him nuts.

Toss in that off-the-charts hot kiss he and Hattie had shared and he was really a goner. Being anywhere near her without touching her was proving incredibly hard.

Which was why when Hattie finally came home at 1:00 a.m. on a Tuesday night, he all but pounced on her when she walked through the door—at least, verbally. Physically, he kept his hands to himself. "It's about time you got here. Don't you have employees without kids who could take over your late night shifts?"

She froze midway through the process of removing her bulky coat. "Maybe you're not familiar with how businesses work, but if I pay out more in salaries than I take in, that's not a good thing."

"You know what I mean." He returned to the living room to pick up where he'd left off reading an online article about infants' strong sense of smell. "If you're hungry, I figured out a fairly decent pork-chop recipe. Left a plate for you in the fridge."

"Thanks."

He was trying. Why couldn't she?

Might be childish, but he refused to even look her way while she banged and clattered through the kitchen. She acted as if she was furious with him, but why? What the hell had he done other than bend over backward trying to make her life easier?

He hadn't even helped her with taking her coat off— not out of a lack of courtesy, but because he feared what the seemingly simple act of touching her may unleash.

Once the microwave dinged, she removed her plate to park at the kitchen bar with her back to him.

Really? She was going to sit there, eating his food without saying a single word? Okay, no more Mr. Nice Guy.

He got up from the sofa, rounded the counter to face her and braced his palms on the granite countertop. "Am I so repulsive that you can't even look at me while eating the meal I prepared?"

For the longest time, she stared at him, then had the gall to laugh—but it wasn't her ordinary laugh; it was more in the range of a guffaw with snorting and side-tears. "I'm sorry, but you sound like a housewife."

"Glad you think it's funny. I'd like to see you sit here, caring for two babies day after day. I'm going out of my mind."

"I can tell." Sobering, she toyed with her green beans. "Me, too. Sorry, I haven't been sharing the workload around here."

"I could give two shits about laundry or burping, but I could really just use a friend. So many guys on my team have kids and they ramble on about how great it is. Maybe I'm approaching this whole thing in too clinical a manner, but as cute as Viv and Van are, when I look at them, I see what their parents did to me. I loved Melissa. Alec was like a brother." Hands fisted, he slammed them to the counter. "Being back has stirred up all this crap I thought was behind me, you know?"

Boy, did she know. Hattie knew all too well what Mason meant, only in her case, it wasn't anger rising from the deep, but so much more. More than anything, she longed to take his hands, unclench his fingers, then kiss them one by one until his anger faded.

"The more I'm around the girls, caring for them, showing them *genuine* love every day, the more I realize this is no joke. But how can I love them when thinking about how they came into this world brings me nothing but pain? Nothing—save for losing my mom—has ever hurt as bad as Melissa and Alec's betrayal."

"Well…" Sighing, she pushed her half-eaten dinner aside. "Lucky for you, you're a short-timer in this whole thing. Even though I have no right, part of me is seriously ticked off at you for even thinking of leaving. Don't get me wrong—I understand you can't just up and quit the navy, but in the same respect, my mind's reeling. I know my folks will eventually come around, but in the meantime, I've got a sharp learning curve in raising these two on my own."

"For the next couple weeks, you don't have to. So how about I help you figure out the hourly logistics of infant care and you help me deal with the touchy-feely side of once and for all getting over your sister."

Hattie extended her hand for him to shake. "Deal."

When he pressed his palm to hers, shivery awareness danced through her, striking a humming chord of attraction low in her belly. How long had she wanted more from him than to be only friends? How long would the memory of the next precious two weeks last, knowing once Mason was gone, it might very well be forever?

"You okay?" he asked, still holding her hand.

"Yeah. I'm good." Her voice cracked with emotion and confusion and wistful longing for what she knew could never be.

"You don't look good— I mean…" With his free hand, he brushed away tears that lately never seemed to stop. Sure, grief played a role in Hattie's current emotional roller coaster, but so did unearthing her long-hidden feelings for this man. "You're pretty as ever, but what do I have to do to help you not look so sad?"

What did he have to do? *Everything.*

Hold her, kiss her, never leave. But honestly? Not only were the odds of all that occurring about as likely as a palm tree sprouting in the front yard, but she owed it to herself to once and for all forget her lame childhood fantasies of them being together and finally get on with her life.

As for their kiss? She *really* needed to forget that!

Chapter Eight

"Good morning, sleepyhead." The next morning, for once, Mason was awake before the girls wailed for room service. In the short time he'd been with them, he'd already seen developmental changes. At nineteen weeks, they were all about exploration, and when he entered their room, Vivian was studying a stuffed frog that shared her crib.

Vanessa was still snoozing.

Sunlight streamed through windows overlooking majestic mountain views.

Vivian caught sight of him and whimpered.

He scooped her into his arms. "Don't start, munchkin. It was a long night and I don't need you making this an even longer day."

Her smile took his breath away.

"Think that's funny?" Cradling her, he tickled her belly.

As much as he kept telling himself he was immune to the girls' charms, he feared many more encounters like this may lead to him having his heart broken all over again by this fresh crop of Beaumont girls.

"Hey…" Hattie stood at the room's threshold, yawning and rubbing her eyes. "I promised myself to be out of bed early enough for you to sleep in."

He grinned at his drooling charge. "I'm used to early mornings with no sleep." Talking in a goofy voice to coax

Vivian into another smile, he said, "Caring for babies is a cakewalk compared to defusing nukes."

Hattie sighed. "Wish I had your confidence."

"You'll get the hang of it."

"Wasn't I just saying that to you?" Cocking her head, she'd unwittingly sent her long hair into a sexy cascade. Her short flannel nightgown hugged her in all the right places, and exposed even more spots he wouldn't mind exploring. Since when had she stopped being just plain old Hat Trick, and started being sexy?

Laughing, he nodded. "What can I say? The navy taught me to be a fast learner."

After a halfhearted smile, she eased onto one of the room's upholstered rockers, drawing her feet up to hug her miles of bare legs. "No need to get cocky, sailor. I know the basics. Diapering, feeding, baths. What scares me is handling those basics, plus my regular full-time job."

"I thought your mom would be helping?"

"Me, too, but all of the sudden it's like she's checked out. I feel like she's blaming me for Melissa's will. It's crazy."

Mason changed Vivian's diaper. "What about Alec's folks?"

"Since they left for Miami, they're a nonissue." She took Vanessa from her crib. After kissing the infant's chubby cheek, she said, "For all the fuss your grandparents made when they heard I'd be caring for you, where are they now?"

"Wanna see your folks this afternoon? Might make it easier if we go together?"

She made a face. "Do we have to?"

"No. Just thought I'd throw it out there." He approached her with Vivian. "Trade with me and I'll get Van cleaned up." The exchange should've been no big deal, but for whatever reason, for however briefly, Mason appreciated the brush of Hattie's warm, smooth forearms against his. Unfortunately, it also left him craving another kiss. "Anything you want to do?"

She'd returned to her chair, only this time holding Vivian upright on her lap. "Let me run something by you."

"Sure. Shoot."

"At the bar last week, Clementine invited us to a Halloween party."

"Cool. I love Halloween."

There she went again with another frown. "Ordinarily I'd agree with you, but we'd need a sitter and—"

"I'm sure Fern and my dad would help out."

"Okay, well, Clem also brought up Wharf-o-Ween. I always have a huge, kid-friendly booth to represent the bar, and—"

"Wait—" he snorted "—are we talking, like, tequila for toddlers?"

She stuck out her tongue. "I know, it sounds weird, but all of the other wharf businesses participate, so why shouldn't Hattie's? And for the record, obviously, no alcohol's served."

"I get it, but what's your question?" He shifted his weight from his left leg to right, but apparently the movement was too sudden for Vanessa's taste. The baby burst into startled tears. "Hey…" he soothed.

"Never mind. We should probably get these two fed."

"Can't we walk and talk?"

In Hattie's defense, she tried, but once Vivian heard her sister's wail, she started in. Neither quieted until their mouths were too busy with breakfast to scream.

Once they all shared the sofa, Mason exhaled. "Damn, that was intense. If these two are this demanding as babies, I can't imagine them as teens."

He cursed silently as yet again, Hattie's eyes filled with tears.

"Good times." She smiled faintly. "Anyway, what I started to ask was if you think it'd be inappropriate for us to take the girls to the festival?"

He took a moment to chew on that one. "You know, if the twins were older, you could let them dictate what they want to do. With them being so little, the decision's yours."

"Which lands me right back to the heart of my question. Wharf-o-Ween or quiet night at home?"

"Might just be me," he said, "but I'd enjoy the crap out of getting away from this house."

HATTIE'S SIDES HURT from laughing.

Conifer's generic equivalent of Walmart— Shamrock's Emporium—carried a meager, yet fun stock of Halloween masks, costumes and makeup. Mason plopped a giant, green Hulk head on Vivian and surprisingly, far from her being upset about it, she giggled while playing peekaboo, peeping out the mask's eyeholes.

The girls sat in their stroller and Mason held up Vivian's little arms, waving them while saying in his best Hulk voice, "Don't make me angry! You won't like me when I'm angry!"

"Stop!" Hattie pleaded in a loud whisper when people started to stare. "We're going to get kicked out of the store." With a permanent population of just under two thousand, but a seasonal flux that jumped as high as four thousand, Hattie knew a lot of people, but thankfully not everyone.

Vanessa took one look at the back of her sister's green head and burst into tears.

Hattie's heart melted when Mason lifted the sniffling

baby girl and cradled her close. "I'm sorry. I didn't mean to make you angry."

Vivian kept right on giggling.

Hattie crouched alongside her, making sure to keep the mask from covering her nose or mouth.

"How about a halo for you?" Mason perched a heavenly headband on the still-spooked girl.

"Aw…" Hattie fished through her purse for her phone. "Keep that on her. I've got to get a picture."

Just as her camera app flashed, Sophie Reynolds rounded the corner with a pricing gun in hand. She took one look at the cheery foursome and turned right back around, all but running to escape them.

"Sophie, wait!" Hattie removed Vivian's mask before chasing after one of the town's biggest gossips.

"How could you?" Nearly to the checkout, Sophie spun around to face her. "Poor Alec and *your sister* are barely in their graves, yet this is how you choose to pay your respects?"

From behind her, Mason approached. "Sophie—not that it's any of your business, but I've done a lot of research on infant grief and the best thing we can do for these two is provide constant love and support—and yes, maybe even a little fun."

Sophie snapped, "What do you know about grief, Mason Brown? It's no secret why Melissa left you. The poor woman had just lost your child and you—"

"Stop," he said in a dangerously low tone Hattie had never before heard. He shifted Vanessa, holding her protectively against his chest, cupping his hand to her ear, shielding her from the brunt of their confrontation. "Don't you dare make excuses for the inexcusable. If *my* wife needed comfort, she should've come to me—not Alec. And thanks

for remembering that I know all too well what it's like—
having also lost my mother when I was a kid."

Sophie stashed her pricing gun under the checkout
counter, then dashed to the stock room.

The pimple-faced kid behind the register stared after
her.

A muscle ticked in Mason's clenched jaw.

"I'm so sorry she said those things to you." Acting on
pure instinct and adrenaline, Hattie hugged him from behind. In the moment, he was no longer a tough-guy SEAL,
but the little boy she'd once known. He'd been in the fourth
grade when his mom died of cancer. Hattie didn't remember the funeral specifically, but she had sad memories of
what happened after. She'd asked him if he wanted to play
Matchbox cars. He'd said he couldn't. All of his best cars
were gone.

"Where'd they go?"

"To heaven with my mom."

Later, when Hattie had asked her mom what that meant,
she'd explained that Mason had placed his favorite cars in
his mother's coffin.

Patting him, trying to soothe him as she would her
nieces, Hattie swallowed the latest knot in her throat. "I've
never liked that woman. At Melissa and Alec's wedding,
she pulled me aside to ask if I wanted to borrow her shawl
to cover my *inappropriate* strapless dress."

"You're kidding."

Hattie shook her head, but then smiled. "Right after
downing two shots of Johnnie Walker Black, I told her I
like being inappropriate."

Chuckling, he turned and set Vanessa into the stroller
before drawing Hattie into a hug. He kissed the top of her
head. Held her and held her until she felt they'd connected

on another level—an indefinable place that was deeper, and infinitely more meaningful, than just friends.

"Thank you for that," he said into her hair.

"I didn't do anything."

"Sure you did. When it felt like this whole damn town sided against me, you were always there. Still are. And now…" He exhaled sharply. "I wish I could be there for you."

"WHAT DO YOU think he meant?" Clementine asked when Hattie relayed the incident at Shamrock's later that night at the bar. "Could that have been his stab at declaring his undying love?"

"Don't be ridiculous." Hattie filled two draft-beer orders, delivering them to the regulars at the end of the bar.

"Stranger things have happened," Clementine pointed out upon Hattie's return.

"And Bigfoot could kidnap me on my way home, but I'm not going to dwell on it. Sorry I said anything."

Rufus Pendleton, a regular, sat at the far end of the bar and signaled for another beer. "I ever tell you 'bout the time Bigfoot paid a visit to my mine?"

Clementine delivered his order. "Only around ten times, darlin'." She leaned over the counter to kiss his leathered skin.

He blanched, wiping the spot she'd touched.

Hattie had been so stunned by Sophie's cruelty—the pall it'd placed over what had previously been a nice day—that she'd needed to talk it over with her friend. But now? She realized she should've kept her big mouth shut. What Hattie had viewed as a sweet moment, Molly Matchmaker saw as the launchpad for a smoking-hot affair.

What about that lone, spectacular kiss?

Had that been significant? Hattie kept that informational nugget to herself.

After an exaggerated eye roll, Clementine popped a green olive from the garnish tray into her mouth. A lot of bars rarely—if ever—cleaned their trays, but Hattie found that practice disgusting and washed theirs once per shift. "What'd you decide about my party and Wharf-o-Ween?"

When Clementine helped herself to three cherries, Hattie said, "Didn't we have an employee meeting about that?"

Her friend feigned wide-eyed innocence. One downside to sanitary trays was the fact that everyone enjoyed snacking from them. "A meeting about what? Our Halloween booth?"

Hattie gave Clementine's hand a light smack the next time she tried to grab a snack. "Knock it off. And yes, we will be hosting our usual booth, only we're adding a pic of my sister and her husband. I think it'd be nice to remind people to live in the moment because you never know what could happen."

SINCE TREVOR VOLUNTEERED to cover the late shift, Hattie used the free time to stop by her parents' home. She'd brought a foil-wrapped plate of hot wings for her dad and mozzarella sticks for her mom.

Inside, she set the snacks on the entry-hall table, then removed her coat and boots. The place was dark as a tomb.

"Hello?" she called out.

When no one answered, she found the kitchen empty. She opened the door leading to the garage to find her dad's truck gone. Hattie's old room, which her mom now used as a craft room, was also empty. Melissa's room remained much as it had when she'd left to marry Mason. Even back then, Hattie had known she was second best in her parents' eyes and hearts.

The last place Hattie checked for her mom was the master bedroom. She found Akna curled onto her side, eyes wide-open, staring into the darkness. "Mom? Are you all right?"

"What do you think?"

Hattie sat gingerly on the side of the bed. "It was sunny today. Still not quite dark. Wanna watch the sunset? It might make you feel better."

"Don't even try pretending you're innocent."

"Wh-what?" The anger behind her mother's statement stung.

"Sophie told me about your plans to carry on as usual for Halloween. The whole town's talking about your abhorrent, downright scandalous behavior. Don't think Sophie didn't tell me everything you and Mason did down at the store."

"Good grief, all we did was pick up a few Halloween items for the girls."

"Didn't sound so simple to me. I remember your sister's letter—the way she made it seem like she was playing match-maker. I know there's more to it, and now you're cozying up to Mason like he's your boyfriend, but he'll always belong to your sister. I'll bet you're loving that big, old house of hers, too, huh? And her new car? Melissa had everything you ever wanted, and now that she's dead, pretty as you please, tied up with a neat bow, you've had her whole life handed to you on a platter."

The horror of her mother's words caused Hattie to raise her hands to her mouth.

"You should be ashamed." Akna sat up in the bed. "You're an abomination—stepping into your sister's shoes like that."

"I—I don't even know you...." Trembling head to toe, Hattie backed out of the room. She had to get away before she said something she regretted.

"Run!" her mother shouted. "You should run straight to church! Pray for the sin of wishing your sister dead!"

Hattie ran, all right, but in the direction of sanity.

Straight toward Mason, who, at the moment, felt as though he was one of her only friends.

THE NEXT MORNING, Hattie had just finished washing the breakfast dishes when her cell rang.

The babies had long since been fed and were lounging in their playpen. It hadn't escaped Hattie's attention that the girls cried and slept more than they ever had in their mother's care, so times like these, when they seemed content, she especially cherished.

Mason sat at the bar, drinking coffee and reading the paper. "Who's that?"

Hattie frowned. "Mom. I'm sure she's doing better."

On a line filled with static, Akna said, "Did you go to church like I asked?"

"Stop this. You've already lost one daughter. Do you really want to lose another?"

Sobs filled the line.

Part panicked, part incensed, part unsure how to be the adult when the woman she'd looked up to her whole life was obviously falling apart, Hattie said, "Mom, I think you should have Dad take you to the clinic. You're not acting rational."

"You're the one who—"

Unable to bear a moment more of her mother's ranting, Hattie pressed the disconnect button on her phone. "Think it's too early for a beer?"

"That doesn't sound good." He put down the paper.

"Aside from my mother having gone so far off the deep end, she's on the verge of discovering a new continent,

there's the issue of how much I despise living in this fish-
bowl of a small town."

"What happened?"

"Apparently, Clem opened her big mouth about the bar
sponsoring our usual festival booth. Sophie had already
given Mom an earful about our *shocking* behavior at Shamrock's and now it seems everyone's gossiping about what a
disrespectful sister I am. A-and now my mother seems to
think that I'm a little too happy about stepping right into
Melissa's life. Apparently, the only possible chance I have
for changing my evil ways is through plenty of prayer."
Using a paper towel, Hattie blotted tears that lately never
seemed to stop. "H-how could she say that to me? H-how
could she be so cruel?"

"Come here...." Mason stood and held out his arms for
her to step into. She did, and honestly, his strong embrace
felt akin to that first delicious sensation of sinking into a
hot bubble bath. Though her emotions were still all over
the map, physically, she was content. "I'm sure she didn't
mean it. That was her grief talking," he murmured.

"St-still..." she sobbed against his chest, grateful for
his strength when she had none.

"Shh..." He stroked her hair, flooding her with warmth
and well-being. "Everything's going to be okay."

Will it? Because judging by how good Hattie felt standing there in her sister's ex-husband's arms, she couldn't
help but fear at least part of her mother's accusations may
be true.

"What's the matter with them?" An hour later, fresh from
the shower, still embarrassed at having yet again emotionally bared herself to Mason, Hattie entered the nursery to
find baby bedlam.

From where he sat on the floor, holding the two girls,

he shrugged. "I found this lullaby CD I thought they might like, but within the first couple minutes of it playing, they both flipped out. Think Melissa played it a lot? And they're wondering why she's not here?"

"Wouldn't surprise me." Hattie turned off the haunting music she'd heard her sister sing to the girls, then joined the trio on the floor. She took Vivian from Mason, holding her close, rocking her back and forth. "I'm sorry, little one. I know you miss your mom and dad."

She looked up to find Mason hugging and patting Vanessa.

Having recently been the recipient of his strong, reassuring hold, Hattie knew his brand of comfort to be effective.

In a few minutes, both girls had calmed. The silence was a relief. "That was intense."

"No kidding. Makes me wonder—how many other memory bombs are around here, just waiting to go off?"

Fingers to her throbbing forehead, she rubbed.

"Anything I can do for you? It's been kind of a crappy morning."

"You think?" Her half laugh didn't begin to cover how much she still hurt from her mother's call. Witnessing her nieces' grief only compounded Hattie's troubles.

"Come on. What can I do to make all three of my girls smile?"

His girls? She met his perilously handsome gaze, warning herself not to read anything other than friendly concern into his statement. It didn't matter that lately, the man had become her lifeline. Not only was he leaving in a week, but just like the perfect house and beautiful babies, he didn't belong to her. Would *never* belong to her.

"Hit me," he teased. "There's gotta be something selfish you've been craving."

She tilted her head back and smiled. "All right, if we were in an idyllic, happy universe, I think I would very much enjoy a pedicure and brownies."

"Done and done."

"Really?" She arched her right eyebrow. "And just how do you propose to make that happen?"

"First…" He set Vanessa on the carpet before standing, then scooping her back up. "We're going to traipse down to that ridiculous home theater and pop in a sappy chick flick."

"I'd rather watch an action-adventure."

"Or that…" He kissed the crown of Vanessa's downy head. What did it mean that Hattie craved another of his kisses so badly for herself that she could practically feel the one her niece received? "Then I'm going to make that brownie mix I stashed in the grocery cart when you weren't looking…"

Hattie frowned, but not too hard.

"And while the brownies are baking, I'm going to paint your gorgeous toes."

"What in the world would you know about nail polish?"

He sobered. "I may be a bit rusty, but when my mom was sick, she always asked me to paint her nails Candy Apple Red. It made me proud to be able to make her smile." Outside, the day was cloudy, but even in the nursery's dim light, Mason's eyes shone. "Will you let me do the same for you?"

Swallowing hard, she nodded.

Then she wished for the power to not only forget their lone kiss, but to stop craving another.

Chapter Nine

To say Mason felt horrible for what poor Hattie was going through would be the understatement of the century. They'd lived together for nearly two weeks, and in that time, he felt as if he'd had a front-row seat to watching her world crumble.

For as long as he could remember, she'd been his little buddy. His pal. But lately? He'd felt the stirrings of something more. Not only the desire to see where another kiss might lead, but a fierce protective streak was emerging regarding her and the girls. Yet as much as one part of him couldn't wait to return to base, another part dreaded leaving Hattie and the twins on their own.

The morning of Wharf-o-Ween, while his dad and Fern watched the girls, Mason hauled the heavy plywood pieces to Hattie's carnival-style booth from the bar's dusty attic. Thankfully, their latest snow had melted and the sunny day already boasted temperatures in the balmy forties.

While Hattie wiped dust from everything with a damp cloth, Mason used his shirt sleeve to wipe sweat from his brow. Only he wasn't sweating from exertion, but the excellent view of her derriere and thong teaser visible every time she knelt to scrub a board. "You owe me big-time. I would hardly call this the quick job you described."

"If I'd told the truth, would you have still offered to

help?" The grin she cast over her shoulder tugged at his heartstrings. Lord, she'd grown into a fine-looking woman.

He couldn't help but smile back. "You've got me there. What's next?"

"Help me get these pieces clean, and then we get to start assembling."

"Swell..." After three hours of torturing himself by keeping his hands off Hattie and busy with power tools, they'd constructed an Old West–styled ringtoss game, with plenty of fun toys and candy they'd purchased at Shamrock's for kids to win as prizes.

Hands on her sexy-full hips, she stood back to survey their work. "Looks pretty good."

"And who do you have to thank?"

"You." She ambushed him with a hug, then stepped back as if checking herself. Part of him wished she hadn't. She smelled good. Like fabric softener and the strawberries she'd sliced for their breakfast. Being with her not only felt comfortable, but exciting—like jumping out of a perfectly good airplane for a stealth night mission. Hattie still held all of the qualities he'd enjoyed about her while growing up, but this new, adult version of her was even better. She had an edge to her. That kiss ignited a curiosity that left him wondering what might happen—not that anything needed to happen. "I appreciate everything you've done."

"Aw, shucks, ma'am..." He tipped an imaginary cowboy hat. "It were my pleasure."

"Layin' it on a little thick, cowboy?"

"Probably so, but considering the looks the good Lord failed to give me, I have to rely on purdy words to impress the ladies."

That earned him a playful swat. "Fish for compliments much?"

He just smiled, realizing he liked the rise in his pulse

that their playful banter had created. Only, considering he practically had one foot on the plane that would fly him from town, was that really a good thing?

THAT NIGHT, as Hattie manned the game booth with Mason, Princess Vivian took one look at a kid dressed like a werewolf and that was all it took for her to break into a wail.

Vanessa, on the other hand, stared up from her perch in the crook of Mason's right arm with wide-eyed wonder.

"Want to take this one," he asked, offering Hattie Vanessa, "while I get Viv calmed down?"

"Thanks." She watched with awe as all it took to calm her niece was Mason's magic touch. He sang, but with a local rock band playing and children laughing, she couldn't make out his words, only that the sentiment was apparently sweet enough for Vivian to find comfort nestling into the crook of his neck.

By feeding time, when the girls had grown cranky again, Mason handled that situation, too, by carting both girls off to the peace and quiet to be found in her old apartment.

After a thirty-minute crush of ghosts and vampires and even a pint-size Britney Spears, Hattie finally got a breather, only to have her dad wander up to the booth.

"Looks good," he said with a faint smile.

"Thanks. The bar was too busy for any of the guys or Clementine to help out, so Mason did most of the work."

"Where's he now?"

"He's got the twins upstairs for a quick bottle and diaper change."

Her dad's expression read confused. "Why aren't you handling that?"

"Honestly? He's better at it. The girls adore him."

Scowling, he shoved his hands in his pockets, nodding

toward the plastic pumpkin she'd set out with Melissa and Alec's wedding picture attached, along with a sign asking for donations to Conifer Search and Rescue, who'd so valiantly tried to save her sister. "That's nice."

"I figure every little bit helps."

He nodded.

"How's Mom?"

"Still in bed. Hope the doctor won't give her any more sedatives. She's not in her right mind."

Hattie wasn't sure how to respond. The pain of her mother's accusation was still too fresh.

"I heard about what she said to you. Didn't like it." He took a few seconds to stare at her sister's photo. "You have to know it's her grief that has her talking crazy. She'll come around."

Wiping tears from her cheeks, Hattie nodded.

"Everyone's smiling again." Mason stepped around the booth's corner, holding both bundled-up infants in his arms. "Oh—hey, Lyle."

"Mason."

The two men seemed wary of each other. Hattie remembered a time when her father had considered Mason his son.

"How's Akna?"

Not one to easily share his emotions, her father said, "She'll pull through."

"Gotta be tough." Mason settled the twins into their stroller.

For Hattie, the tension between the only two men who'd ever meant anything to her was becoming unbearable. Hoping to smooth things over, she suggested, "How about you and Mom come for dinner on Sunday?"

Mason hovered behind her, and as Hattie awaited her

father's answer to her impromptu invitation, she appreciated her friend's silent support.

"It's awfully nice of you to ask," Lyle said, "but I don't think your mom's up to it. Soon, though. We'll get together real soon."

"Sorry," Mason said after her dad left as quietly as he'd arrived.

"It's okay," she said, even though nothing could be further from the truth. More than anything, she longed to turn around and lose herself in the strength of one of Mason's hugs, but what would that do except prove Hattie was the despicable person her mom and Sophie and apparently the whole rest of the town believed her to be.

"Turn right back around," Clementine said to Hattie when she arrived for her usual Saturday night shift. "I told you I've got you covered for tonight so you can come to my party."

Hattie made a face. "I'm not really in the mood to play quarters or beer pong."

Clementine waved off her concerns. "This is a grown-up party. I'm planning for Pictionary and dancing in the living and dining room and *Halloween I, II* and *III* on TV."

"What?" Hattie feigned shock. "No *Friday the 13th?*"

"Think that would be better?" She reached for an olive.

"What have I told you about eating the bar garnishes? And for the record, I'm messing with you. Sounds like a good time."

"Then you and Mason are coming?"

Hattie set her purse behind the bar. "Not sure if you're up on current events, but my sister just died. I shouldn't even be talking about going to a party."

"What was Wharf-o-Ween?"

"That was different." She poured herself a Coke. "I

wanted the girls to hear laughter again. Plus, my dona-tion pumpkin raised over four hundred dollars for search and rescue."

"Oh—so it's all right for the girls to laugh, but not you?"

"They don't know any better. But it's been suggested I do."

"By who?" Clementine crossed her arms.

"Lately, I feel like everyone. You know Mason and I had that run-in with Sophie, and now my mom has to-tally lost it—not that I blame her. I'm upset about my sis-ter, too, but—"

"Wait. What else happened with your mom?"

Hattie relayed her mother's most recent call.

"Ouch." Clementine winced. "I'm sorry she went off on you, but you can't internalize her grief. Everyone has to deal with this in their own way. Melissa didn't give you the luxury of crawling into bed for a month. Yes, mourn your sister, but her girls also need you to celebrate her."

THE WHOLE RIDE HOME, Clementine's words refused to leave Hattie's head. Was she taking her mother's grief too per-sonally? To be fair, having no children of her own, Hat-tie couldn't begin to fathom the depth of her mother's pain. Yes, Hattie was sad, but no comparison to what her mother—or Alec's—must be going through.

Upon entering her sister's home, thundering racket alerted her that she'd find Mason and the girls in the movie room.

Sure enough, while Mason reclined in one of the sump-tuous leather chairs, the girls lounged on their play pads. Vivian stared in wonder at the colorful screen on which *Finding Nemo* played out. Vanessa focused her attention on gumming a cloth-polar-bear rattle.

"Hey," Mason called upon seeing Hattie. "Not that I'm complaining, but what're you doing home?"

After depositing her purse on one chair, Hattie sat in the one nearest Mason. "Clementine informed me we are going to her party. If your dad and Fern don't mind sitting, do you feel up to it?"

He groaned. "How many of the old crowd will be there?"

"Actually, I doubt many. Clementine and I are more the blue-collar type."

"Doesn't matter. If that's what you want to do—" he paused the movie "—I'll call Dad."

Just like that, Hattie had a date for Halloween—not just any date, but the man of her dreams. So why didn't she feel happier about the situation? Why was she allowing her mother's hateful accusations to ruin a fun night out—a night Hattie deserved?

Why? Because if Hattie so much as touched Mason, then Akna's horrible claims about Hattie's lack of morals, and lack of loyalty to her sister, would be true.

"REALLY?" HANDS ON her hips, scowl firmly in place, Clementine appraised Hattie's and Mason's impromptu costumes. "I shouldn't even let you in the door. What are you supposed to be?"

"Duh. TV antennas." Hattie brushed past her and, in the process, adjusted the tinfoil cap Mason helped make.

He passed their hostess the tray of pumpkin-shaped cookies they'd picked up at the grocery store on the way over. "Clever, right?"

Clementine just shook her head.

The party was already in full swing with classic Kid Rock booming from the stereo speakers. The house was decorated with orange and black streamers along with dozens of orange light strands. Hattie knew most of the twenty or so guests, but had to introduce Mason to a few of the men and women who were new to town.

Joey and Dougie were spending the night at Clementine's mom's place.

Hattie and Mason played Pictionary for a while, but when they lost every round, and Hattie found herself forcing good cheer, she was glad when Mason offered her a beer, then asked if she wanted to get some air.

"Good idea," she said, standing alongside him on the two-bedroom home's back deck. Just being near him produced a fierce longing for a forbidden, elusive *more*.

"No offense, but you looked a little out of it in there."

She laughed. "You've got a good eye."

"Anything in particular got you down?" He rested his forearms against the railing, glancing back at her, moonlight kissing his handsome features. The mere sight of him took her breath away, transported her to a magical place where there were no worries, only the two of them. "Or just our situation in general?"

"Remember how when we first got to Melissa and Alec's place, the game room still had the remnants of Craig Lovett's birthday?"

"Sure."

"Obviously, this is the first party I've been to since then, and it just occurred to me how different that night would've been had any of us known what was to come." When her eyes teared up and the familiar knot in her throat formed, Hattie forced herself to stay strong. The worst had already happened. Her job now was to steel herself for whatever the future held.

Mason groaned before tugging her in for a hug. "Hat Trick, if there's anything the navy has taught me, it's that tomorrow's never guaranteed. You have to take what today gifts you and be good with it."

"I know...." Clinging to him, knowing he'd soon be leaving, too, she fought not to lose herself in fears of her uncertain future and of being a single parent to her sister's girls. "But it's easier said than done."

He tenderly placed his hand beneath her chin, forcing her gaze to meet his. "Come Friday, when I sign away my rights to your nieces, I need you to know that has nothing to do with you. I might be back on base, but I'll only be a phone call away."

"Th-that's supposed to make me feel better?" She wrenched herself free, yanking off her stupid tinfoil hat, wadding it in a ball and tossing it out into the yard.

"I hoped it would. Last thing I want you thinking is that I'm abandoning you." She turned her back on him, but he stepped up behind her, curving his hands over her shoulders. "What your sister did—leaving her kids to me..." He sighed. "What the hell was she thinking?"

A question Hattie asked herself every day.

TRUTH BE TOLD, by the time Friday morning rolled around and Mason stood in line at Era Alaska with Hattie to board their short flight to Valdez, he was more than a little relieved. The sooner this custody thing was behind him, the better off he'd be.

Ever since the party, Hattie had been a sullen mess. The twins weren't much better. As for *his* mood? It ranged between sympathy for what Hattie was going through to annoyance over her shutting him out. On the surface, she was polite, but he knew her well enough to recognize the camaraderie they'd shared before the party was long gone.

Thank God for Fern and his dad watching the twins, because after the week he'd had, he could use the time away.

His dour companion mumbled, "Just when I think life can't get worse."

"What's wrong?"

She held up her cell to show him a weather-radar image. "What're the odds of this storm affecting our flight home?"

"Nil." Had circumstances been different, he'd have pulled her close for a reassuring kiss. "Stop making up worries, and let's try to enjoy our day."

"Impossible. The closer I get to officially being a single parent, the more my stomach hurts."

"What do you expect me to do? Even if I wanted to, I can't just up and quit. I can ask for more leave, but at some point, I will want to finish at the very least my current enlistment."

"I know. And I'm sorry to be dwelling on this. Consider the subject dropped."

"Oh, no, you're not going to launch a—"

"Sir." The attendant leading them to their plane gestured for him to follow. Just as well, considering their circular argument had been getting them nowhere.

He waved at Hattie to lead the way, and then noticed her gray complexion. He felt like kicking himself. She'd just lost her sister to a plane crash. Why hadn't he suggested they take a ferry?

"Hey—" He clamped his hand around her upper arm. "I didn't even think of the implications of you getting on a plane. We don't have to do this—at least, you don't. Let me sign the papers on my own."

"Benton advised us to present a united front."

"What if I advise you to spend your afternoon soaking in a nice hot bath?"

"Do you ever shut up?" Her legs wobbled visibly and she planted both hands on the rails to mount the prop plane's short set of stairs.

About a dozen snappy comebacks came to mind, but it wasn't the right place or time for sniping at each other. If she refused to get off the flight, the least he could do was ensure she knew he was there to lean on—assuming that at this point she even wanted his support.

She chose to sit in the back. He followed, ducking in the cramped space.

Only three other passengers were on the flight, and they occupied seats near the front.

As the pilot cleared them for takeoff, Hattie's complexion grew more waxen.

Mason reached across the narrow aisle and took her hand. She tried valiantly to rip it from his, but he said in a low tone, "Knock it off. I might be leaving Sunday afternoon, but for now, I'm here, and I *will* help you through this."

From that point through the duration of the flight, Mason held her hand, and she let him, and when the sun broke through the clouds just before landing, dowsing them in brilliant warmth and light, he couldn't help but wonder if Hattie's sister was sending her own form of comfort.

But when the aircraft's wheels touched ground and Hattie dropped his hand as if he'd burned her, his own nerves set in. Was he doing the right thing? Even if a small part of his conscience said he wasn't, what could he do about it? At the very minimum, he owed the navy a solid two years. And regardless of what she'd put in her will, he owed Melissa nothing.

What about Hattie?

What about that kiss you can't forget?

He ignored the voice in his head. Three weeks earlier, he'd rarely even thought of her. So why did thoughts of Hattie—and her adorable nieces—rarely leave his head now?

Chapter Ten

"Relieved?" Hattie asked Mason on the cab ride from the courthouse to the airport. The storm she'd shown him earlier had yet to materialize, which was a relief as the sooner he got away from her the better.

"No." He stared out the window at the hodgepodge of hangars and less-than-tourist-worthy homes. The judge had been ahead of schedule, and signing away his parental rights and monetary claims to any of Melissa's and Alec's possessions had taken all of ten minutes. "Look, we're about three hours early for our flight. Let me at least buy you a decent meal. Steak? Sound good?"

She shrugged. "If you want."

It beat the hell out of sitting with her at the airport for three hours. "Ah, sir," he said to the cabbie, "would you mind running us back to that two-story steak place with all the antlers?"

At the restaurant, Mason paid the driver and got his business card so they'd have his number for their return trip.

A hostess seated them at a table near a crackling fire. The antler theme went a little overboard with antler candle holders, chair backs and even an antler railing on the stairs leading up to the inn's few guest rooms. What space on the walls that wasn't graced with antlers, there were framed head shots of celebrity guests.

A country singer crooned over a radio in a thankfully low volume about his cheatin' ex.

Once the waitress left with their drink orders, Mason said, "I don't know about you, but I'm thinking this place could use a few more antlers."

For the first time that day, Hattie cracked a smile. "You think?"

Their Jack and Cokes arrived, and after ordering two steaks, Mason was fresh out of conversational fodder.

First downing a good third of her drink, Hattie said, "Mom dragged me and Melissa up here for a quilt festival a couple years ago. We ate here one night." Down went another third. "It was pretty good."

"Glad to hear it."

"Quilting's never really been my thing. Had more fun the next year when Dad and I stayed over at the Robe Lake Lodge. We took a charter—caught a salmon shark. Took nearly ninety minutes to reel him in." Her drink was gone. "He'd never admit it, but I'm pretty sure Dad's still jealous."

"Don't blame him."

"You see our waitress?" Considering at two in the afternoon, the dining room only had three other guests, it wasn't too hard to find the young woman seated in a corner booth, texting on her cell.

"What do you need?"

She waved to the girl and held up her empty glass, jiggling the ice.

"You didn't eat breakfast or lunch. Think you might wanna pace yourself?"

"This time Sunday, you'll be long gone. Why do you care?"

He took the empty glass from her. "Because I care about you."

"Bull."

The waitress delivered Hattie's second drink.

"This time next week, you won't even remember my name." Down went her latest third, as did the zipper on her red sweater. "It's *waaay* too hot in here. Oops," she said when going low enough to expose a seriously sexy black lace bra.

An instant, damn-near-painful erection had him shifting positions. He didn't need reminding about his recent dry spell. He sure as hell didn't want to even ponder the notion of ending it with an innocent like Hattie.

Pointing to her bountiful breasts, he made a zipping motion. "You, ah, might want to assess that situation."

She glanced down only to wave off his concern.

He leaned across the table, doing the job himself by raising her zipper to a respectable position.

"You know," she said in a perfectly sober tone, "this situation sums up my life. I've always been seen as the good girl. Everyone's always zipping me up." Her second drink emptied. "Well, guess what? I'm tired of being good. And now, here I am mom to two kids and I didn't even get great sex before getting knocked up."

Mason choked on his drink, then did a quick check of the room to make sure no one had overheard Hattie's complaint. "The guys you've been with haven't been doing it right?"

"Not even a little bit…." She took a moment to ponder her revelation. "Pretty sure this is a sign I need more liquid courage."

"Courage for what?"

"The whole single-mom thing, but mostly, I'm drinking however much it takes to remind me to keep my hands off of you."

She tried signaling the waitress, but he managed to snag her arm before she got the woman's attention.

"Would it be so bad?"

"What?"

"Putting your hands on me?"

She snorted. "It'd be the worst thing in the history of the world. Don't get me wrong, you're tastier than hot apple cobbler, but I'm not going to take a single bite—not even a lick."

The thought of her licking him sent a fresh jolt to regions better left ignored. What Mason had intended to be a simple celebratory meal had suddenly become a sexually frustrating adventure. By the time the waitress brought salads, then their steaks, snow fell so hard that the parking lot vanished from the windows' view.

He pulled up radar on his phone to find the snow had not only arrived ahead of schedule, but stronger in intensity than forecast.

When a tipsy Hattie damn near stabbed herself with her steak knife, he cleared his throat and asked, "Um, Hat Trick, how about letting me cut your meat for you?" Her all-too obliging come-hither smile did little to erase the image of her *assets* that had been burned into his retinas. Up close and personal, her floral shampoo reminded him of their many summer outings.

He may have married Melissa, but he'd had fun with Hattie.

Guilt from the realization had him retreating to his own personal space.

The waitress stopped by with the dessert menu.

Mason ordered cheesecake.

"Do you have beefcake?" Hattie asked with a snort.

After clearing his throat, Mason tugged his phone from his pocket. "I'll check on our flight."

"Why?" Her seat faced the river-rock hearth and its mounted moose head.

"Look behind you."

She did and closed her eyes. "You do know Alec and Melissa's accident was because of bad weather?"

"Yeah." His dad told him the visibility had been fine when the couple had left Conifer, but roughly fifty miles south of Anchorage, they'd run into a snowstorm. One more glance out the restaurant's window had Mason doubting they'd be going anywhere soon. "Let me give Era a call."

"Well?" Hattie asked when he disconnected.

"Nothing's going in or out for a while." Snow already had day quickly fading to night.

With a groan, she dropped her head to the table. "Just when I thought I wouldn't have to resist you much longer…"

"Hang tight." Lord, what he wouldn't give to break her resistance, but his dad had raised him better than to take advantage of a girl who'd had a few too many. Mason finished off his cheesecake, then pushed back his chair. "I'll grab a couple rooms. We'll get a good night's rest, then regroup in the morning. I'm sure Dad and Fern won't mind staying with the twins. Sound good?"

She may have nodded, but judging by her crestfallen expression, he'd had dogs more excited by the prospect of spending more time with him.

Five minutes later, Mason returned, but not with the news he'd expected. He dangled a key from a canoe key chain. "Hope you're not a blanket hog, because they only had one room."

HATTIE WOKE FROM a three-hour nap to find Mason on the king-size bed beside her, pillow propped behind him. A woman on *Wheel of Fortune* had just snagged a Hawaiian vacation, but he didn't seem all that excited. If anything, his handsome profile struck Hattie as stoic—resigned to riding out the storm with her when he'd probably rather be with a flashy blonde.

Save for the TV's glow, the room was dark. Wind howled just beyond closed drapes. The old building shuddered from occasional gusts.

Most ordinary folks would be battened down for the duration, but typically, the word *ordinary* and Alaskans didn't match up. Judging by the muted bass and laughter coming from downstairs, a blizzard party was in full swing.

Hattie envied the happy game-show contestant. "What would you give to be lounging on a Maui beach right about now?"

His unexpected smile raced her pulse. "Sleeping Beauty awakes." He tugged a chunk of her hair. "You were a handful at lunch."

"Yeah?" She yawned. "I don't remember much past my third drink."

"Likely story," he teased. "Come here."

He snagged her around her waist, tugging her close, landing her head atop his chest—exactly where she'd wanted to be, but knew she shouldn't.

"I like tipsy you." He kissed the top of her head. "Your honesty was quite the turn-on."

She groaned, squirming to get away, but he tugged her back.

"My head's fuzzy on your exact phrasing, but at one point, I'm pretty sure you admitted you'd like to lick me."

Groaning even louder, she covered her flaming face with her hands. "Stop."

"I would, but you pretty much seared that image into my brain. Then there were your asparagus tricks…"

"Stop…"

"Nah…" Lifting her up to him, he kissed her real slow, doing plenty of searing with his lips. When she groaned, he pulled her closer, easing his big, rough hand under her sweater. Being with him like this felt so natural, so right, so— What was she thinking?

"Mason, no—" She pushed him away, then tidied her hair. "We can't do this. It's wrong."

"Why?"

Images of her mother and beady-eyed Sophie Reynolds flashed before her, as well as her radiant sister on the long-ago day she and Mason married. "It just is. I can't—won't—be the kind of woman who—"

"Actually lives her own life?"

That very question was what had led her to drink. After Mason signed the forms releasing him from his parental duties, he'd essentially stepped one foot out the door of their shared life. The thought of no longer playing house with him, exchanging brief touches with him or even lingering looks had sent her running straight for liquid courage.

Oh—she'd be leading her own life, all right—her very-much-alone life!

"Ha-ha." She slid off the bed, straightening her sweater in the process. "You're so *not* funny."

"Just keepin' it real, Hat Trick." After a yawn and stretch, he asked, "Hungry?"

"Not really." *Yes.* When wasn't she? But thinking of her latest abandoned diet would hardly stop her downward emotional spiral.

"Mind at least sitting with me while I grab a burger?"

"Sure. Help me find my shoes and we'll head downstairs."

What a difference a few hours made. The place was packed.

The only seats to be had were a couple stools at the bar.

While Mason called his dad to check on the twins, Hattie called her own establishment. Clementine had long since gone home, but Craig and Trevor reassured her all was well and that they'd also been slammed with folks seeking an excuse to party through the inclement weather.

"Wanna beer?" Mason asked.

"Yes, please."

After agreeing to share onion rings, Hattie raised her longneck brew. "How about a toast?"

"To what?"

"There are good ships and wood ships. Ships that sail the sea. But the best ships are friendships. May they always be."

Mason said, "I'll drink to that."

They clinked bottles.

Desperate to avoid the elephant in the room—his imminent departure—Hattie said, "Since you've been in town, we've talked about babies and wills and more death than I care to remember, but you've said nothing about what's really going on with you. Have a good group of guys you hang out with? A girlfriend?"

He reddened. "My guys consist mostly of my SEAL team. My best bud, Calder, just got married and had his second kid." After a long swig of beer, he turned introspective, swirling his bottle against the smooth wood bar. "For the longest time, I was pissed at him for turning to the Dark Side. Your sister really did a number on my head." He drew a deep breath. "As for the second part of your question— the longest relationship I've had recently was a gallon of milk I forgot to toss before leaving for Afghanistan. Can you believe she stayed with me for six whole months?"

"Not sure whether the similarity of our love lives should make me laugh or cry—although I did have a guy stick around for that long. Constantine..." She finished her beer. "Great in bed. Hopeless at keeping a job." Mortified by what she'd just admitted, she pressed her hands to her flaming cheeks. "Could I sound like any more of a money-grubbing hussy?"

"Don't sweat it." He finished his drink and signaled the bartender for two more. "I happen to very much like hussies."

Before she could even wonder if she should take his statement at face value, he winked. "I get it. You're over thirty and entitled to a satisfactory roll in the sack—hell, we all are. As for the cash? Seems to me a man's work ethic speaks volumes about his character."

"True..." Mason's had always been top-notch. "Melissa used to bitch a blue streak about you working too much. I lost count of the number of times I reminded her you were working for her—your future kids."

"See? I love that you get that—you've always gotten that. You're good people, Hat Trick. Wise beyond your years."

"I try." Fresh drinks arrived.

The dining room furniture had been compressed, allowing for a makeshift dance floor. The roaring fire, combined with gyrating bodies, upped the room's heat—both figuratively and literally. Lights had been dimmed to almost nonexistent and she found herself embracing the dark.

It made her bold.

Made her forget herself and her worries and everything but this moment with the only man she'd ever wanted.

Hattie lowered the zipper on her sweater, then fanned

herself with a napkin. "You'd never know it's probably ten degrees outside."

He laughed, then held out his hand. "I love this song. Let's dance."

Rod Stewart's "Da Ya Think I'm Sexy" morphed into a slow and sexy Def Leppard number that had Hattie pressed against Mason in an anything-but-friendly manner. Swaying to the music, they abandoned themselves to the fire's hedonistic glow, and he settled his hands low on her hips. Was it the fire's heat or his touch that had her skin flush and thoughts dizzy?

Everyone knew blizzard parties were like Vegas. What happened at the party stayed at the party.

Mason eased his hands under her sweater and up her bare back as she pressed her hands to his chest, fisting his shirt when their gazes met in a way they never had before. How many times had she stared into Mason's eyes? She liked to think she knew him inside and out—that she'd always known him, but never like this.

The song ended and another came on. Still slow, but with Justin Timberlake's painfully sexy vibe. She'd always associated his music with the pretty people—the glamorous party set who'd hung with her sister—but tonight, with a blizzard raging outside and her hair swinging loose and wild, with Mason's wicked hands sliding up her sides, beneath her bra, skimming her breasts' side-swell, she felt pretty. Wanton and wicked. All grown up and, for once in her life, refusing to back away from what she wanted.

He angled his head as if planning to kiss her.

Panic seized her, stopping her heart, then racing it to a frightening degree. What was happening? This was Mason. Her sister's boyfriend—her husband. Her *ex*-husband.

Not asking permission, Mason's hands were out from beneath her sweater to cup her cheeks, pulling her close for a kiss she'd waited a lifetime for. His lips were firm, yet supple, drawing her in, only to tease her by backing away.

She had never been more out of breath—out of control. She couldn't have stopped kissing him if the room caught on fire.

He played his teasing game until the end of the song, but then things got serious when he grasped her hand and led her away from the crowd to the stairs.

There, he took things to a whole new level, lowering her to sit on the nearest step, then arching her back, kissing her, haunting her with the sweep of his tongue—for he had to know regardless of where the night led, she'd never forget his kiss. His faint taste of beer and raw masculinity.

He hovered over her, pressing his swollen need against her. "You okay with taking this upstairs?"

She somehow found the strength—the courage—to nod.

Chapter Eleven

Safely hidden behind their closed door, their urges broke free. Hattie didn't even try pretending being with Mason in every way a woman could wasn't exactly what she wanted.

She ripped at his shirt just as he did away with her sweater. Like a blind woman seeing the sun for the first time, she reveled in gazing at his every muscular nuance and groove. Where her body was soft, his was hard. Honed from she couldn't even imagine how many hours of working out.

Cloaked by darkness, she forgot to care about what he thought of her body in favor of savoring his every touch.

He backed her against the nearest wall, but it turned out to be the door leading into the bathroom. It didn't matter, as he slowed things down while impossibly racing her pulse all the more.

"You're beautiful…." His words were a ragged whisper.

"No…"

"Shh…" He was back to exploring, kissing her abdomen and still lower until he was between her legs and she buried her fingers in his hair, abandoning herself to a swift climax that built into another. His touch transported her to a place where anything was possible, where dreams really did come true.

By the time he'd left her to grab a condom from his

wallet, she thought she'd been ready for him, but nothing could've been further from the truth.

Eyes closed, the sheer beauty of his motion, of the two of them finally uniting as one, knotted her throat to the point she was no longer able to hold tears at bay.

"Hey...want me to stop?" He paused, which prompted her to press her fingers into his back, urging him to continue—to never stop.

"No. Please..." Her mind was too addled for speech.

"What's wrong?"

"Please, Mason...don't stop."

He braced his hands against the wall, giving her an opportunity to dance her fingertips along his impressive biceps.

"What else can I do? You're crying."

"Lately, I'm always crying. It's not a big deal."

"Hattie..."

She kissed him, hoping to convey the depth of her riotous emotions through her actions. "Th-this is a big deal for me—huge. Trust me. I want this—us—more than you'll ever know."

"Well, all right, then..." Mason struggled for thought, let alone words. He had never seen a more beautiful sight than Hattie standing before him, naked, shyly smiling, unflinchingly meeting his gaze. "Wanna take this to the shower?"

"Sounds a little wild," she said with a giggle. "I like wild. D-do you?"

"Hell, yeah.... As long as you're sure."

She turned on the water. "You think too much. You've also apparently been away from Conifer too long. How could you forget the rule about blizzard parties?"

"I didn't. Trust me, I'm all for getting buck-ass wild tonight, then forgetting come morning. But, Hattie, I'm not willing to do it at your expense. You were crying." He wanted to hold her gaze, but lacked the strength when she'd presented herself like a womanly buffet. He drew her to him, so damned relieved he hadn't botched things up.

"In case it escaped your notice, lately I'm always crying. But this time—" she drew back to gift him with the sweetest kiss "—my tears were happy. More than anything I want to be with you. I've always wanted to be with you. If my parents knew, they'd permanently disown me, but for now—tonight—no one ever has to know besides me and you."

"And you're okay with that?" He searched her dear face, those chocolate eyes.

She nodded.

"Sweet. Let's get busy." To once and for all dispel any concerns about her weight, he backed her against the wall, lifting her, urging her arms around his neck and her legs around his waist. "Wanna go for a ride?"

WHEN HATTIE woke to use the bathroom, then settled into an armchair, though it was still dark, she could tell the storm had passed and enough moonlight reflected off the snow to afford her a mesmerizing view. Sleeping Mason was a sight to behold. The wall heater worked a little too well, meaning that after making love a third time, he'd fallen asleep on his back. The sheet only covered his midsection and left leg, leaving the rest of his godlike physique on display.

If she weren't sore in places, she wouldn't believe their shared intimacies had even happened.

But they had.

As a realist, she knew being with Mason changed nothing. He'd still leave bright and early Sunday morning and she'd still raise her nieces on her own. She'd never been a fairy-tale girl; rather, she lived more in the realm of Cinderella before the ball. But now that she'd had her one, sparkling night, no matter what other tragedies fell her way, she'd finally had her chance to be a princess. And it'd truly been a magical affair.

Mason stirred.

On her feet, she rummaged through her purse for the bottle of water she'd stashed earlier that day. She took three long sips.

Upon her return to the bed, Mason mumbled, then kicked the sheet from his right leg. Whatever he dreamed of seemed fitful.

Should she wake him? She recalled once reading never to wake a sleepwalker, but she'd never heard any rules on standard dreamers.

When his moaning resembled pain, she touched his shoulder. "Mason? You all right?"

He thrashed his head. "No. No."

"Mason? Wake up." She nudged him again, only this time slightly harder.

With a start, his eyes opened, his gaze unfocused, and for a moment he seemed lost. "Melissa?"

Hattie froze. No way had he said what she thought she'd heard. Moments earlier her happiness had been hard to contain, but now she shrank inside herself, only just realizing the depth of her mistake. She knew he wasn't still hung up on her sister, but that didn't change the fact that they'd shared a significant past. So significant that Melissa still popped up in his dreams—or nightmares…

Hattie had no business being with him. Nothing good could come from anything they shared.

Eyes again closed, he fitfully kicked his legs. "Baby? Is that you?"

Though Mason drifted back into peaceful slumber, for Hattie, sleep never came.

At 5:00 a.m., she tired of trying. Instead, she dressed in the previous day's clothes, ran her brush through her tangled hair, then wrote a hasty note for Mason, telling him that when he woke, she'd be in the lobby.

For now, she needed coffee, pastry and the space to process her thoughts—however dark they may be.

MASON WAS SORRY Hattie hadn't been in bed when he woke. After the wild night they'd shared, he wouldn't have minded kissing her good-morning.

How crazy was it that after all these years of being friends, they'd discovered something more. On the flip side, how depressing was it that he was soon leaving. Somehow, he had to make her understand that despite that fact, their night hadn't been purely about sex. She'd always meant the world to him and still did. He wasn't quite sure how she fit into that world, but he'd worry about that another day.

For now, he took a quick shower, toweled off, then tugged on clothes still in a rumpled heap from where they'd been tossed the night before.

Damn, Hattie had been a closet hottie. No more calling her *Hat Trick*—more like *hellion.*

Downstairs, he found the sun-flooded dining room restored to its former sedate pace. Two business-types sat at tables, reading newspapers and drinking coffee. Then there was Hattie, seated cross-legged on the sofa in front of the fire, reading something on her Kindle. She'd crammed her long hair into a messy ponytail, and even from a distance, he could tell she wasn't her usual self.

"Hey…" He kissed the crown of her head before sitting next to her. "Quite a night, huh?"

Her smile didn't reach her bloodshot eyes.

After placing his hand possessively on her thigh, he asked, "Everything all right?"

She nodded. "I'm glad you're here. We should head for the airport. Our flight leaves in just over an hour."

"Wish you'd told me sooner. Might've been nice to share breakfast."

She shrugged.

He glanced over his shoulder. "Mind telling me what I'm missing? In light of, you know…last night. Your cold shoulder's kind of freaking me out."

"Good. Then we're even." Before he had the chance to ask what that meant, she was on the phone with the cab-driver. Upon hanging up, she stood. "We're in luck. He's only a few minutes away."

"Swell. That'll hopefully give you just enough time to explain what the hell's wrong with you? Is this about me leaving?"

She shook her head. "Can we please just get back to Conifer? Last night was a mistake. We both know it."

"Are you kidding me?" After a quick check to make sure the other guests were ignoring him, he took Hattie's hand, easing her fingers between his. "Last night was not only hot, but opened my eyes to a whole new part of you. You're like Hattie, but better. I have to get back to the base, but I was thinking, for the holidays, how about you and the girls fly out for a visit? Wouldn't that be fun?"

There she went again with her waterworks, but not before jerking her hand free. "You have no idea, do you?"

From outside came a honk.

"No idea about what?" Mason asked. He'd grown seriously tired of this game.

"Come on. That's our ride."

"What about the bill?"

"Already paid."

She was midway to the door when he caught her by her upper arm, spinning her to face him. Under his breath, he said, "Damn it, Hattie, tell me what's wrong or we'll stand here all day."

"You called out for Melissa, okay?" She took a tissue from her purse, blotting her eyes. "After spending the whole night making love with me, turns out your subconscious prefers my sister."

While he stood dumbfounded, taking in the gravity of what Hattie had just said, she was already at the inn's door, tugging it open.

Mason chased after her, and when she slipped on snow-covered stairs, he almost caught her, but hadn't been quite fast enough to break her fall. The way she landed on her right arm didn't look good. In his line of business, he'd seen a lot of men get hurt, and to him, this looked potentially serious. "Are you okay?"

"Fine," she insisted, brushing off his attempts to help. "Please, leave me alone."

He at least opened the sedan's back door for her. When she'd climbed in, he closed the door and walked around to the other side.

With no desire to air their dirty laundry in front of a captive audience, he waited until after they'd checked in for their flight to pick up where they'd last left off.

"So, about last night…" he said in a quiet corner of the airport terminal. "Are you honestly blaming me for something I said in a dream? Hell—" he raked his fingers through his hair "—I don't even remember what it was about."

"Must've been good. After a lot of groaning, you said her name, then called her 'baby.'"

"You're being crazy," he had no problem telling her. "I

can see you being upset we didn't use a condom or that
I hogged the blanket, but this?" He laughed. "You, of all
people, should know how much pain your sister brought
me. You, on the other hand, have always been the one who
made me smile."

Whether she liked it or not, he leaned in to kiss her, and
damn if her whole body didn't seem to exhale in relief.

"Hattie, I'm sorry if I accidentally hurt you. But the
God's honest truth is that—for me, anyway—last night
was amazing, but that's where it has to end. You and I both
know sheer logistics make it impossible for anything life-
altering to happen."

She nodded. No matter how much his speech hurt, his
words made sense. "Thank you for the apology. And I to-
tally get what you're saying. Our already-gossipy town
would have a field day should they ever have an official
report of us being together." She forced a breath, then
swallowed the knot in her throat. "Not gonna lie, hearing
you call out my sister's name shattered my heart in about
a zillion tiny pieces, but what I was too punch-drunk on
fun sex to realize was that, like you said, last night can
never be more than that—fun. Pleasure shared between
two consenting adults at a blizzard party."

Leaning forward, he rested his elbows on his knees.
"Want a coffee?"

She shook her head.

Due to so many flights having been canceled the previous afternoon, the airport was buzzing that morning.
After Mason stood in an endless line for standard black
coffee, it was time to board their flight.

Once again, Hattie's complexion paled as she reached
her seat, but this time she had no interest in holding his
hand. Which just so happened was fine by him.

The sooner he got away from her and back to Virginia Beach, the better off he'd be.

THE FLIGHT LASTED thirty-five minutes, and it took another fifteen of his father's agonizingly slow driving for Mason and Hattie to reach Melissa and Alec's house, where Fern sat with the girls. An added hour of polite small talk just about did him in.

On a trek outside for more firewood, his father asked, "What's with the chill between you and Hattie?"

"Long story."

"Good or bad?"

Mason laughed. "Little of both."

His dad grunted. "What time you want me to fetch you for the airport in the morning?"

"Six, please."

"You got it." His dad's rare hug couldn't have come at a better time. Mason didn't feel right about going, but he sure as hell knew it would be a huge mistake staying.

By the time Mason and Hattie had the house to themselves, he couldn't tell if she was still upset with him or something else was wrong. Her color was seriously *off,* and she'd winced when picking up or even holding either baby.

"You all right?" he finally asked when they both happened to be in the kitchen.

"I'm fine. But as soon as I wash these bottles, can we talk?"

"Here, let me help." Alongside her at the sink, he took one look at her swollen right hand and turned off the faucet. "Are you kidding me?" She tried turning from him, but he'd already reached for her left arm. "You're seriously hurt, aren't you?"

"It'll be fine. I want to apologize for this morning. Last night was so... And I just..."

"I get it. Apology accepted. Right now, since your arm looks too swollen for me to even roll up your sleeve, I'm taking your sweater off, okay?"

She nodded.

Last night he'd unzipped her sweater for purely selfish reasons, but he now found himself in a wholly altruistic position, tensing when Hattie winced with pain. Her arm had turned a dozen shades of purple and that told him it had to be broken. "Jeez, woman, were you ever planning to do something about this?"

"I figured after a couple days it'll feel better."

"Uh-huh." He tossed her sweater on the counter, wishing he had her top off under more fun circumstances. He ushered her to the sofa. "Wait here while I grab you a T-shirt. Then we're running to the clinic."

"That's not necessary. Besides, after being crazy this morning, I want to do something nice for you. Maybe wash your clothes?"

From the stairs, he said, "How about once we get home you take a nice nap? Then we'll call it even."

"Could you have misread the X-ray?" An hour later, Hattie sat on an exam table at Conifer Clinic. Mason had stayed in the waiting room with the twins, and from the muted cries, she guessed he wasn't having fun, either.

Dr. Murdock laughed. Five years earlier, the town had paid her med-school loans in exchange for her services. Turned out she was a great fit. "Sorry, hon, but I'm afraid you're looking at a minimum of six weeks in a cast. The good news is that we just got in a really great pink."

Hattie groaned. "Not only am I not really a girlie girl, but I don't have time for being even temporarily down one arm."

"Well, I can't help you find more time, but I do have lots

of colors. Red? Orange? Black? Christmas is just around the corner. How about green?"

"Guess that'll work."

Thirty minutes later, sporting her two-ton green arm and a prescription for pain meds, Hattie found Mason in the crowded waiting room, jiggling a baby on each of his knees.

He looked up only to catch sight of her and frowned. "Told you so."

She stuck out her tongue.

He winked. "Don't threaten me with a good time."

"Hush. I'm in pain and just realized no meds for me."

After settling the girls in their carriers, he joined her at the checkout desk.

In the sunny parking lot, amid mounds of melting snow, he asked, "Why can't you have medicine?"

"Do you think it'd be a good idea to be loopy while single-handedly caring for two infants?"

"Hadn't thought of that."

He set the carriers alongside the SUV while opening Hattie's door. "Hop in. I'll load everyone else."

"Thanks." Because he wouldn't be around much longer to help care for the girls, Hattie closed her eyes, soaking in the warm sun while he tackled the chore of fastening them into their safety seats.

Everything would be all right. As long as she stayed positive and worked hard, she was fully capable of raising the twins, healing her family and running the bar. The cast wouldn't even slow her down. Piece of cake.

They were midway back to the house when Mason asked, "What would you think about me extending my leave?"

"What? Why?" Her heart skipped a beat at the mere prospect of him sticking around. Trouble was, the more she was with him, the more she realized he needed to go—not just for his job, but her peace of mind. The doctor had reminded her the holidays had nearly arrived. Hattie had to somehow get her family back to normal and she sure couldn't accomplish that when Mason's mere presence made her feel anything but!

"You obviously need help. Since there's no way my mind will even be on my work if I'm worried about you, I figure why not see about extending my leave? Great idea, right?" He aimed his killer, white-toothed grin in her direction.

With the memory of what he could do with that mouth all too fresh in her mind, she tried covering her face with her hands, but instead, conked her nose with her cast. Could this day get any worse? Whether Mason left in the morning or after New Year's made no difference. Sooner or later he would go. And even though she had no business wanting him to stay forever, she did. Feared she always would.

An even bigger worry was the one Mason's own subconscious had proved real. The fact that in his sleep he'd cried out for Melissa told Hattie that no matter how hot their night had been, in his mind, she'd always finish a distant second to the way he'd once felt about her sister.

And she deserved better than being a guy's second choice. If she couldn't be Mason's top pick, then she'd prefer not having him at all.

She pasted a smile on her face and said, "You're sweet to think of me, but the girls and I will be fine. It's probably for the best that you go."

Chapter Twelve

Mason wasn't sure what to think of Hattie's negative reaction to his suggestion that he stay. She obviously needed the help, so what was her problem? "If this is about last night…"

"No, not at all," she assured him. "I just think it's best to get on with the inevitable. Last night was…well…"

Freaking incredible. "I get it. Yeah, you're probably right." If she'd been hoping for a different reaction, her expression gave nothing away. Had she truly been that unaffected by what they'd shared? "I'll leave as planned."

"Good."

Her attitude was really pissing him off. How could she be so cavalier? Or was it an act? If so, why did she feel compelled to lie to him, of all people? They'd known each other forever. If there was anyone she could be her true self with, he hoped it'd be him.

But then, why should she feel allegiance to him? The genuine friendship they'd shared might as well have happened a hundred years ago. Had her sister's death created what was essentially an artificial reality, thereby forcing a reunion? A reunion that was actually an illusion?

Was Hattie the only one of them smart enough to call last night for what it had been? A blizzard-party hookup between old friends who were better off *just* friends?

Ignoring Hattie's protests, he swung by the pharmacy, filling her prescription so at the very least she'd have relief for tonight.

Back at the house, she tried helping get the twins inside, but he fended her off. "Go on in and take your medicine."

"I'm perfectly capable of handling the girls, you know?"

"Yep."

"Then let me—"

"Hat Trick, please…you're only stuck with me for one more night. Do me the favor of letting me take care of you till I'm gone?" He held her gaze, silently signaling her to chill. Leaving her and the twins was already hard enough. Leaving under these circumstances made him feel like the world's biggest jerk.

"Sure. Whatever. Toss me the keys, though, so I can at least unlock the door."

Finally in the house, Mason corralled the twins in their playpen, then got Hattie settled on the sofa, bringing her a Coke, her medicine bottle and her cell so she could ask one of her employees to cover her shift. "Need me to bring you a few crackers? You probably shouldn't take it on an empty stomach."

"Thanks, but I'll be fine."

He started to make a fire, but instead took a seat on the cold stone hearth. The chill seeped through his jeans, but had nothing on the deep freeze that had settled over Hattie. "You ever talking normal to me again?"

"Thought I was?"

He snorted. "Right."

"Sorry. I'm not trying to be difficult. I'm just hurting and mad at myself for being in such a rush this morning that I fell."

Mason wanted her to keep talking—admit she was also

upset by his leaving. Instead, she made an awkward grab for a movie magazine Fern had left on the coffee table.

"Where do you think you'll be this time tomorrow?"

Her question caught him off guard. Truthfully, he was surprised she even cared. "Jeez, I guess I'll still be in the air. I leave Anchorage at 9:25 in the morning, but don't land in Norfolk till 10:15 at night. Gonna be a long day."

"But a good one." Her faint smile tightened his stomach. Damn, he wanted to kiss her. "When I was a kid, I always dreamed about traveling. It's gotta be exciting, going all over the world like you do."

"It is—was—but it's not often the navy takes us any-where sane people would want to be."

"I suppose...."

There was so much he wanted to say to her, but where did he begin?

Never did Mason think he'd be happy to hear either of the twins cry, but in this case, he was glad for the distraction. "Guess it's dinnertime, huh?"

"Want me to help?"

Hopefully, his glare conveyed how serious he was about her resting.

"Come here, you little bugger." With Vivian in his arms, Mason set about making bottles, finding comfort in the routine. When she turned her tear-filled baby blues on him, he melted. "You're going to grow into one helluva heartbreaker."

From the playpen, Vanessa wasn't happy about her sister hogging the attention.

"Just a sec, sweetie. I'm almost finished, then heading your way."

In his peripheral vision, Mason caught a flash of movement from the sofa to the stairs. He turned back in time to see Hattie vanish in the hall. "What the..."

HATTIE REACHED THE bathroom just before retching into the commode. Why hadn't she listened when Mason told her to eat something with her medicine? What else had he been right about? Wanting to stay?

She'd wanted so badly to agree with his plan, but what was the point?

Seated on the tub's tile edge, she rested her elbows on her knees. More than anything, she wanted to call out to Mason, ask him for a cool rag, but in the morning he'd be gone and she had to once again learn to not only live on her own, but be happy about it.

Twin cries rose faintly upstairs.

Seconds later, Mason stood in the bathroom's doorway. "You okay?"

Nodding, she drew strength from just knowing he was near. "Hate to admit it, but you were right about those crackers."

"Sorry." As if reading her mind, he took one of Melissa's designer washcloths from the towel rack, dampening it before holding it to her forehead.

"Thanks. I should've listened, huh?"

From downstairs, the wailing grew louder.

He knelt, kissing the top of her head. "You gonna be all right if I leave you for a sec? I'll grab those two and bring them up here to feed them."

"I'm fine. No need to hurry." *Or even come back to me at all.* Because his presence only worsened her pain.

The babies soon enough quieted, but then she heard what sounded like Mason talking on the phone. Creeping from the bathroom to the stairs, she eavesdropped on his conversation.

"Yes, sir....Thank you....Same to you, sir."

Who was he talking to? His dad?

"I'll be sure and let you know....Yes, sir. Thanks, again."

She'd never heard him call Jerry "sir."

One of the twins whimpered, so she headed that way to help. And maybe get a better feel for who Mason was chatting with. His whole demeanor had changed. He'd deepened his voice and squared his already-broad shoulders.

For a split second, her mind's eye returned to their shared shower, and the way those shoulders had looked all soapy and wet. Mouth dry, she willed her pulse to slow and her mind to get out of the gutter.

"Who was that?" she asked, striving for a casual tone.

"My CO." He scooped a sniffling Vivian from the playpen, teasing, "What's the problem, princess? Your appetizer wasn't adequate?"

The infant's giggle only further degraded Hattie's foul mood. The twins had already lost their parents. Having bonded with Mason, would they mourn his loss, too?

He knelt for Vanessa, and then, once he held both girls, he took their bottles from the counter before heading for the sofa.

"Want me to take care of them so you can pack?"

His slow grin destroyed her. "Didn't I tell you to rest?"

"Since when do I ever do what you tell me?"

Laughing, he said, "Good point."

Seated alongside him, she used her good arm to take Vanessa. "Wanna hand me her bottle?"

He passed over a bottle, and they finished feeding the girls. Darkness had fallen and she shivered from a sudden chill. Her medicine made her eyelids heavy.

After tugging an afghan from the back of the sofa to drape over her lap, Mason said, "I'm going to give these two monkeys a quick bath, then put them to bed. If you're still awake, want to watch a movie or just make out in front of a fire?"

"Excuse me?" If she'd thought for one second he was serious, her choice would be all too obvious.

"Just kidding. See you in a few."

"Mason, if you need to pack, I can handle tub time. It's not a big deal."

"Relax…" There he went again with his grin. "We have all the time in the world."

"Yeah, if you don't sleep a wink. Didn't you ask your dad to be here at six?"

"Guess I should give him a call, huh? Tell him his taxi services are no longer needed."

Eyes narrowed, she asked, "What're you talking about?"

"Wouldn't you like to know?"

In no mood for teasing, she snapped, "Actually, yes, I would."

"Jeez, Hat Trick, chill. I won't need Dad for one simple reason—I'm not leaving."

Had she heard him right? "Wh-why?"

"Isn't it obvious? You've got a broken arm, these angels need pretty much around-the-clock care and selfishly," he murmured, and dropped his gaze only to then pierce her with his direct stare, "I wouldn't mind further exploration of that sexy genie we let out of the bottle."

While he exited up the stairs, Hattie leaned her head back and sighed. *He's staying.*

Which meant her sanity would soon be going…

ALMOST TWO WEEKS later on a snowy, extra-busy Friday afternoon, Hattie struggled using her free hand to stock the bar. With Mason available to take the baby monitor at night, she was able to take her pain meds for sleep. During the day, however, her pain was light enough for her to soldier through.

"Why are you even here?" Clementine asked. "You know we banded together to cover your shifts indefinitely."

"Thank you. I love you guys for that, but I'm all right. Just a little slow. Besides, I seriously needed out of the house." Or, more specifically, away from Mason. Aside from his occasional X-rated double entendres, he'd been a perfect gentleman, not even delivering a peck to her cheek. Which should've come as a relief. Ha!

The more space he gave her, the more she craved jumping into his arms.

"Sure was good of Mason to stay. Your dad told me he's not leaving till you get your cast off, which is, like, what? Just after New Year's?"

"Somewhere around there." Hattie stretched her back, taking a break from the chore of stocking the glass-front fridge.

"You've gotta be relieved."

"I guess." Thank God for the fridge's cool air dowsing her flaming cheeks. If Clementine learned Hattie's dirty secret, she'd never hear the end of it.

"Could you be any more apathetic? The guy has no legal reason to be here, but turned his whole life upside down to put himself at your beck and call."

"It's not like that. For the most part, we share watching the twins."

"Then there must be some other reason he's staying."

"Ask me," grizzly old Rufus Pendleton said from down the bar, "the man's got it bad for you. Not a good thing, considering past history and such."

"Keep out of it," Clementine snapped to their regular.

"Just sayin'…." He finished off his shot and signaled for another. "No good can come from a union between those two. For him, it'd be like shackin' up with a ghost. For her, steppin' right into her big sister's fancy shoes."

"For the record, Rufus," Hattie said, "there's nothing going on between Mason and me." She tried ducking back into the fridge, but too late. Her friend had already spied her using a collapsed six-pack case as a makeshift fan.

"Oh. My. Gosh." The size of Clementine's grin rivaled the half-mile wonder of Conifer Gulch. "You two totally did the deed?"

"Shh!" Hattie held her finger to her lips, eyeing Rufus. "Don't be so crude!"

"Excuse me, did you make *sweet love?*"

Hattie refused to answer. Damn her stupid, flaming cheeks!

"You've liked him forever. But you've got to be freaking out. Your mom's already having a tough time with Melissa—no way is she going to be okay with you sleeping with her ex."

Hattie released a relieved sigh when Rufus and his latest shot headed to the nearest pool table.

"Thanks for reminding me." Hattie started unloading the next case. "And for the record, we were only together one night. It's not happening again."

"Is that what you really want?"

Hattie sat on the stool they kept behind the bar for when it was slow. "I don't know what I want, other than for things to go back to normal."

"Sweetie," Clementine said, with a hand on Hattie's forearm, "I'm no expert, but after suffering a loss like you have, I think you have to fight your way to a new normal. Thanksgiving's coming, then Christmas. For those babies, you have to get your family back on track. If that means officially welcoming Mason back into the fold, then your mom's just going to have to deal."

"Yeah…" Was now the time to admit her deepest fear

had nothing to do with her mom's disapproval and every-thing to do with the fact Mason still dreamed of Melissa?

"I'D BE LYING if I said I wasn't disappointed you're not gonna be here for Christmas." Since Hattie was at her bar, Mason navigated Shamrock's, using the twins' stroller as a shopping cart for detergent and trash bags, while listening to his SEAL friend "Cowboy" Cooper whine for the past five minutes about losing his drinking buddy, even if only temporarily. "I swear to God, if you get hitched like Calder and Heath, I'll lose what little respect I have left for you."

"No worries," Mason said with a laugh, maneuvering down the chip and soda aisle. "Just as soon as Hattie's cast comes off, I'll be back on base."

"She's your ex's sister, right?"

"Yeah. We're just friends, though. No big deal." Unless Mason counted the number of times a day his mind replayed their wild night.

"Glad to hear it. Thanks for the reassurance, man."

With another laugh, Mason said, "No problem."

They swapped stories for a few more minutes, Mason retelling Vivian's Halloween scare and Cooper relaying his latest wild night with a blonde. How times had changed. Used to be they talked about weapons, video games and women—not necessarily in that order. Never had babies made it into the conversational mix—unless they were bitching about how nauseating it was for their married friends to blather on about their kids.

After finishing his call, Mason found lightbulbs and a new movie magazine for Hattie—who claimed she didn't read them, but had devoured Fern's cover to cover. Oh—and while he was thinking about it, he also grabbed more brownie mix.

Facing the girls, he asked, "Can you two think of anything else we might need?"

Though he'd have a long wait before they officially said their first words, both girls had grown more adept at babbles and coos.

"Ahhh..." Vivian hummed while gumming her rattle.

Vanessa gurgled while staring up at the store's fluorescent lights.

"She needs all of that, huh?"

Vivian performed a few excited wiggles.

Thanksgiving bouquet displays graced both sides of the checkout. Mason took one for Hattie, but then also for Akna and Fern. Hattie never talked about how much the rift between her and her mother bothered her, but she'd visited twice the past week and both times returned home crying. He could only imagine what Hattie might have to say concerning his olive-branch attempts. She'd tell him to stay out of it. Mind his own business. Everything would be fine.

All of that was well and good, but it'd been a long time since he'd had a traditional Thanksgiving—the last decent one had been with his friends Calder and Pandora. He couldn't even remember the last time he'd celebrated with his dad. If pressed, it'd probably been the year Melissa left him.

By God, if making Hattie smile meant hand delivering folks to her Turkey Day feast, he'd do it.

He cringed to find Sophie manning the sole checkout line. "Flowers?" she asked with eyebrows raised.

"For Hattie and her mom—and Fern."

The old bat had the audacity to snort. "You do know folks are talkin'? Doesn't seem natural for you to be with your dead ex-wife's sister."

"Thank you for your opinion, Sophie. Next time I'm

looking to ruin my day, I'll be sure to make this my first stop."

Mason ignored the pit in his gut that Sophie's condemning glare had left and loaded up the girls and his purchases, then drove toward Hattie's childhood home. "You gals ready to see Grandma Akna?"

Vivian did her happy bounce, but Vanessa rubbed her sleepy eyes.

"Ladies, let's make this an in-and-out mission. We'll hand Grandma her flowers, then remind her Melissa might be gone but you're still here."

And please, God, let Akna be more welcoming than Sophie, because his patience with busybodies was wearing mighty thin.

Chapter Thirteen

"Mom, please," Hattie pleaded, "at least tell me what I can do to help. I know you miss her, but you can't spend the rest of your life in bed." She eyed the row of prescriptions on her mother's nightstand. After her confession to Clementine, the last place Hattie had felt like staying was the bar, but her snap decision to check in on her parents wasn't turning out much better.

"I'll be fine," her mother assured her.

"Then prove it by coming over on Thanksgiving. You do know it's next week?"

"Honey, it's too soon. It's not appropriate to celebrate holidays with your sister gone."

Hattie counted to five in her head. She lacked the patience to get all the way to ten. "Thanksgiving isn't known for loud music and balloons. It's about family, and sharing what we're thankful for."

"I have nothing." She rolled over to face the wall.

Hattie wanted to go off, reminding her mother she still had a husband, daughter and two granddaughters who needed and loved her, but she sensed nothing she said would break the drug-induced fog.

After drawing the quilt her grandmother had made higher on her mother's slim shoulders, Hattie left the room.

She found her father stoking the fire.

"Heard you two talking," he said. "Have a good visit?"

"No. In fact, it was awful. You have to get her off of the sedatives."

"I know." Seated on the hearth with his shoulders hunched, her father looked defeated.

"Just take away the bottles. She hasn't been on them long enough for her to be addicted, but if she doesn't stop soon, she could be. Please, Dad, don't let it get to that point."

He nodded.

To make sure he'd heard her, she went to him, clutching his hands. "I want to have a big Thanksgiving with all the trimmings, okay? We'll use Melissa's fancy dining room and china. She'd like that. You know how she used to love to entertain. And instead of being morose about missing her, let's celebrate her life, okay?"

Sighing, he said, "You make it sound so simple, but for your mom and me, it's different."

What else could she say? Since losing Melissa, life had been *different* for her, too, but she didn't have the luxury of hiding. If her sister hadn't asked Hattie to raise the twins, would her mother still be in this funk? Or had the will's directive stolen her purpose?

Dragging in a fortifying breath, Hattie said, "Okay, well, I'm going to go. I'm sure I'll see you before Thanksgiving, but in case I don't, please bring Mom over around noon. I'll fix some appetizers—plenty of the stuffed mushrooms and hot wings you love from the bar—and we'll have dinner around two. Sound good?"

"Sure. We'll be there."

Hattie wished with all her heart she believed him.

She'd just made it to her car when Mason pulled in behind her. Even seeing him through the windshield made everything feel better.

"What are you doing here?" she asked when he rolled down the driver's-side window.

He took a cellophane-wrapped fall bouquet from the passenger seat. "I grabbed these at Shamrock's. Thought your mom might like one to help get her in the holiday spirit."

His thoughtfulness blasted a hole through the defensive wall she'd built around her heart. "You're kind to think of her, but she's dead to the world. I'll take them in and leave them with Dad."

"You sure? Seeing the girls might make her feel better."

"Yep. I'm sure." Recalling her mother's spaced-out stare, Hattie didn't think fireworks accompanied by turkeys dancing beneath a candy-corn rainbow would restore her usual cheery demeanor. Deep down, she was scared for her mom—and for herself. Hattie had already lost Melissa; she couldn't bear losing her mom, too. Knowing she was on borrowed time with Mason already hurt bad enough.

"All right, how about we meet back at the house, then you climb in with us so we can all take flowers to Fern?"

Eyes tearing, she asked, "Does the navy know their big, tough SEAL is actually a teddy bear?"

"Hat Trick, you can't go around staying stuff like that. You'll ruin my manly reputation."

On her tiptoes, she recklessly kissed his whisker-stubbled cheek. "Sorry. I promise not to let it happen again."

What she'd have a tougher time with was honoring the promise she'd made to herself to keep her distance from this amazing man.

As if fate agreed with Hattie's decision to back off from Mason, Sophie pulled her Impala into the driveway she shared with Hattie's parents. Judging by her sour expression, not only had she seen the kiss, but she'd disapproved.

"Are you sure you didn't give me a cup of salt instead of sugar?" The night before Thanksgiving, with Mason's help, Hattie was attempting to make her grandmother's pumpkin pie, but something about the texture didn't seem right.

"Pretty sure," Mason said. "Taste it."

"It's got raw eggs."

He rolled his eyes, then dredged his index finger through the mixture. He swallowed and said, "I've eaten worse."

"What does that mean?"

"Just bake it. I'm sure it'll be fine."

The babies had been in bed for an hour and the house felt eerily quiet. "Want me to put on some music?"

"Sure." He washed the measuring spoons. "What's next on the menu?"

"Pumpkin bread. Mind getting the walnuts from the pantry?"

She turned on Alec's pricey Bose stereo. He'd subscribed to satellite radio and she hadn't yet called to cancel, so she used the remote to find a soft-rock station.

Mason emerged from the pantry, wearing a grin. "Wanna dance?"

"No, thank you. Clearly, the last night we danced, I'd had way too many beers."

"Uh-huh…"

He'd wedged behind her and settled his hands on her hips, swaying them in time to the music. His actions, his body heat, the sexy smell of his breath when he nuzzled her neck made Hattie shiver. "Stop. We need to bake." *And I can't go down this road with you again. It's too dangerous to my heart.*

"Really? You'd rather bake?"

No. "Yes."

"What if I did this?" He spun her around real slow, kiss-

ing her neck, her collarbone, the indentation at the base
of her throat.

Her breathing hitched. Desire pooled low and achy in
her belly. *Never stop.* "You *have* to stop."

"Okay, but what if I accidentally did this…" He slid
his tongue in a tantalizing trail down her chest and into
her T-shirt's deep V. As if that weren't torture enough, he
skimmed his warm, rough hand under her thin cotton T,
following her waist's inward curve.

"Mason…" She wanted him so bad. Knew being with
him again was the worst thing she could do. No good could
come of them being together. *"Please…"*

"You don't have to beg," he teased. "I'd be happy to
kiss you." He tugged out her ponytail holder, freeing her
hair. After easing his fingers beneath her black waves, he
pressed his lips to hers, stealing every shred of her good
judgment in the process.

Somehow, he was then dragging her T-shirt over her
head and then she tugged at his shirt. Last time they'd been
together it'd been dark or she'd been covered with suds and
then a quick towel. He hadn't seen the real her. Would he
stop once he noticed she wasn't a size two? "Should we
go to my room? Dim the lights?"

"Why?" He paused, then made her die a thousand times
under his slow appraisal. Her bra was simple and flesh-
toned. Nothing fancy or lacy or anything she was certain
his usual type might wear.

"Well…" She licked her lips. "Dim—even dark—is
better."

"I like seeing all of you. Do you have any idea how gorgeous you are?"

"No…"

"Yes. Oh, hell yes." He reached behind her, deftly unfas-
tening her bra, then easing the straps from her shoulders.

Under his appraisal, her nipples hardened. She instinctively tried crossing her arms, but he stopped her, drawing her arms back to her sides. "I could stare at you all night."

Was this a dream? She couldn't be sure, because he was back to kissing her, kneading her aching breasts. Unable to believe any of this was really happening, she closed her eyes, abandoning herself to pure pleasure.

When he fumbled for the button to her jeans, she helped him. Together, they tugged them down. Her plain white panties went along with them and for a moment she stood before him completely naked and stunned. No one but her mirror had ever seen her fully unclothed. Would he think her hideous? The way her hips and thighs were way fuller than any woman's in magazines or on TV?

"I—I can't do this," she said. *Mortified* didn't begin to describe how she'd feel if he rejected her.

He groaned. "Baby, don't do this to me." He'd taken off his own jeans and boxers, leaving no question to the matter of whether or not he was aroused.

A giggle escaped her, but she covered her mouth.

"Think this is funny?" he teased, sweeping her into another heady kiss. "I'm in agony. You're so damned sexy it literally hurts."

"No…" She shook her head.

"Woman, have you ever really looked at yourself?" She'd only just noticed their reflections in the living room's plate-glass windows. With no one around for miles, Mason took her hand, guiding her closer to their mirror images. He knelt in front of her, kissing the belly she thought too round. The hips she believed untouchable. "You're curvy and sexy and soft." Rising, he effortlessly lifted her onto a solid oak sofa table. "I want to bury myself in you, leave you begging for more…"

The shock of his entry was soon tempered by pleasure so intense she lost all sense of space and time. In and out he thrust and her body willingly swallowed him whole. Pressure built and blossomed until erupting into all-encompassing joy.

Breathing heavy, she clung to him, needing a few moments to come crashing down.

He kissed her again, this time deep and slow, sweeping her tongue with his. "How could I have missed knowing you were right here all along?"

She couldn't answer because for her, it'd always been him.

"Relax." Mason stood behind Hattie at the kitchen counter while she added more crackers to her cheese platter. With her sexy bottom pressed against his fly, it was all he could do not to drag her into the pantry and have his way with her all over again. Unfortunately, since his dad and Fern sat only a couple dozen feet away, bickering about whether to watch football or John Wayne, Mason behaved, chastely kneading Hattie's knotted shoulders. "They'll come."

Leaning against him, she asked, "What if they don't? How can they stand being away from the girls? Should I run over there? Check if they're all right?"

"They're adults. They know they're invited." He spun her to face him, wanting more than anything to kiss her worries away. Instead, he settled for a quick hug, hoping his dad and Fern didn't see.

"I guess. But it hurts, you know? I don't understand how they lose one daughter, then make a conscious decision to throw their other one away. Not to mention, their grandchildren."

"Babe, I don't think it's like that at all. Surely, by Christmas, your mom will come around."

"Hope you're right." Had it been his imagination, or

had she held him extra close? Almost as if she'd craved his touch as much as he had hers? "Whatever happens, thanks for your help. Everything looks great—although it's a miracle anything got done."

"Complaining?"

He loved the way she reddened. "No, but—"

Mason silenced her with a kiss.

Stunned, she put her hands to her lips. "You can't do that. Not when we have company. In fact, we shouldn't be doing it at all."

She was right, but that didn't stop him from landing a light smack to her behind when she left him to deliver the tray to their guests.

By the time the turkey was browned to perfection and Hattie had whipped mashed potatoes and candied sweet potatoes, his heart broke for her because Akna and Lyle failed to show. She'd even invited Alec's parents, who were all the way down in Miami. Her hands' slight tremble alerted him to her distress.

Fury didn't begin to describe the malice he felt for the two couples. Ever since learning the contents of Melissa's will, they'd taken out their pain on the one person who'd been just as surprised as them—Hattie. That fact royally pissed him off. Granted, as of late, he might be biased, but she was a good woman. She deserved to have only caring, devoted people in her life.

Which category are you?

His conscience's question hit Mason square in the gut. When it came down to it, when he did finally return to Virginia, at the rate their connection was progressing he stood to hurt her more than anyone. He was married to the navy, and even if he weren't, he'd tried marriage and look where it had landed him. He wasn't sure what kind of relationship Hattie was ultimately in the market for, but he felt fairly certain that once she finally did settle down, she'd expect—she deserved—for it to be for the long haul.

Ignoring what would inevitably be his own role in Hattie's pain, Mason sneaked off to the bathroom to make a call to Lyle.

The son of a bitch couldn't even be bothered to answer.

"Dinner's ready!" Hattie called from the kitchen.

Mason tucked his cell in his pocket, then joined everyone in the dining alcove.

"Your table's pretty as a picture." Fern smoothed the tablecloth. She held Vanessa, who kept making valiant attempts to nab Fern's sparkly barrette. "I've never seen so much bling."

"My sister loved putting on a good show. She bought all the crystal and china on one of Alec's business trips to L.A."

Mason thought all of it a bit much. Give him a paper plate and plastic fork and he'd be good. Toss in a campfire and he'd be even better.

On his way from carrying one of the high chairs in from the kitchen, he noticed a series of silver frames. The dining alcove was a spot in the house he'd never much paid attention to, and now he was glad he hadn't. Picture after picture of Alec and Melissa lined a buffet. Smiling. Hugging. Kissing. Turning his stomach. Why, after all these years, did he still let them get to him?

Maybe because they were the reason he now felt incapable of sustaining any relationship. Because they'd taught him not to trust.

His dad carried in the other high chair and eased Vivian into it.

Though Hattie had set the table for six, only four presided around her delicious-looking spread.

She said a brief prayer, and then they dug in. Save for

the clinking of silverware against plates and the girls' occasional grunts and giggles as Fern and Hattie took turns feeding them pureed pears, all was quiet. The girls had grown a lot in the short time Mason had been with them. Seemed hard to believe they were already eating solid foods.

A couple times, Mason figured when she'd thought no one was looking, he caught Hattie glancing at the empty place settings.

Finally, having had enough of her torturing herself over other people's poor manners, he pushed his chair back and cleared the empty plates. "I don't know about the rest of you, but I could use more elbow room."

"Me, too," his dad said, rising to help.

"Hattie, this turkey is as moist as any I've ever had," Fern noted.

"Thank you."

His dad nodded. "I could take a bath in these potatoes."

"You should probably take a bath in something." Fern pinched her nose.

"Ha-ha." Jerry helped himself to thirds of everything.

The meal wound on, and though Hattie didn't say anything, Mason sensed her mood growing ever more somber. By the time they helped each other serve dessert, she was hardly saying a word.

"You okay?" he asked while unearthing the whipped cream from the overstocked fridge.

She nodded.

Back at the table, Mason took charge of serving. "Who wants pumpkin pie?"

"Heck," his dad said, "I'll have a little of everything."

"You'd better get me some, too." Fern held out her plate. "At the rate he's going, there won't be any left."

Jerry dived for his plate, too, only to spit out his most recent bite. "No offense, Hattie, but this pie tastes like a salt lick."

Chapter Fourteen

Paling, Hattie said, "Mason, you tasted it and told me it was fine."

Yeah, he'd also been distracted. "Honestly, not only have my taste buds been ruined by dousing hot sauce on MREs, but I'm more of a pecan pie kind of guy. I'm not even sure what pumpkin's supposed to taste like." And to prove it, he dived his fork right into the pie's center. He chewed and chewed, and when he couldn't hold his fake smile a second longer, he deposited the bite into his fancy cloth napkin. "Okay, so it might be a little salty, but otherwise, it's pretty good."

"Oh, stop." Hattie tossed her napkin on the table, then dashed off up the stairs.

Fern scowled at both men. "Good Lord, were you two raised in a barn? Poor girl. It's her first time hosting a big holiday. Couldn't you lie? I ate my whole piece."

Snorting, Jerry said, "That's because you're crazy."

"No," she argued, "I have manners. Mason, you'd better go after her. It's not every day your own parents stand you up, then your pumpkin pie sucks." She hacked off a chunk of pumpkin bread, slathering it with butter. "Everything else is real good, though."

Mason followed Fern's advice, charging upstairs. The closed guest room door may have muffled Hattie's sobs, but that didn't help him feel better about the situation. Quiet tears were still tears and he hated knowing she was hurt.

He knocked. "Hat Trick? Can I come in?"

"No! And stop calling me that!"

For a split second he considered respecting her apparent wish for privacy, but then barged in, closing the door behind him. "What's with the waterworks? It was only a pie. And Dad and Fern have eaten damn near every crumb of the other stuff you cooked."

"You're such a man. The pie was just the cherry on top of what has been a seriously awful day. Everything was supposed to be perfect, but nothing went right."

Perched on the bed beside her, he skimmed hair from her eyes. "Funny, because up until a few minutes ago, I thought it's been a pretty great day. I've got you and the girls with me. My dad and Fern. I'm sorry your parents and Alec's chose not to come, but that's their loss."

"You're just saying that to be nice. And don't think for a second I didn't see the way you were looking at all of Melissa's pictures in the dining room."

"Yeah? What about it?" He didn't have a clue what she was talking about. "You sound as nutty as Fern."

"Don't even try pretending you don't know what I mean. You slept with me last night, then today, stared like a lovesick puppy at her and Alec's parade of exotic vacation pics."

"Those? Are you kidding me?" He crossed his arms. "Yeah, I looked at them, all right—in disgust. If I looked sick, that's because I was. I'm sorry those two died, and if this makes me sound like the most heartless ass on earth, then so be it, but the God's honest truth is that to me, those two died the day Melissa left me to marry my so-called best friend."

He stood and moved in front of the window. "Look, you have to forget the past. I don't mean erasing your sister's memory, but the role I once played in her life. Anything I felt for her has been over for a long time. As for me and you…"

"Oh, my God, do you ever shut up? As soon as my cast comes off, you're headed back to Virginia. Last night and what happened in Valdez was fun, but you and I both know it'll never go further than that."

Jaw clenched, Mason tapped his closed fist to his mouth.

"My sister was the dreamer. I've always been a realist." She combed the guest room's designer pillowcase's fringe. "I'll be first to admit our hookup has been a nice surprise, but—"

"Aw, Hattie, you mean a helluva lot more than just a hookup to me. Don't you know that? But circumstances being what they are, I don't have anything else to offer."

"Trust me, I know."

AFTER A FEW semifriendly days, followed by smoking-hot nights, Mason had never been more confused. The second Hattie left for the bar on Tuesday, he called his pal Calder.

"Hey, man, we were just talking about you." One of Calder's kids cried in the background. He and his wife, Pandora, shared an almost-three-year-old boy and a one-year-old girl, as well as her daughter Julia from a previous marriage. Mason figured if anyone could help him figure out how to handle the mess he found himself in, it'd be Calder. "There's a betting pool going on whether or not you're coming back."

"Of course I'll be back. I still owe the navy two years."

"You know enough people in high places to bail if need be."

Mason sorted through the day's mail. "That's not my style."

"Didn't say it was, but I know what suddenly having a kid is like—and here, you have two."

"Not anymore. I mean, yeah, I'm still taking care of them until Hattie's arm heals, but I signed away my custody rights."

"Cooper told us." Yipping competed with kid-cries for loudest background noise.

"Sounds like you've got a zoo."

"Pandora and the kids gave me a puppy for my birthday. It's a Yorkie barely big enough to fit in the palm of my hand. Damn thing pees and craps chocolate-chip-sized turds everywhere, but it's so cute you can't stay mad at it long."

"Sounds like you've got your hands full. Should I call back?"

"Not at all. What's up?"

"Not sure where to even start." His doodling on the back of the water bill took on a frenetic pace. "After what Melissa put me through, never in a million years would I believe I'd be thinking about another commitment, but things have developed between Hattie and me that I—"

"Whoa, stop right there." The connection sounded muffled while Calder yelled at either a kid or dog. "Sorry. Crowd control. Listen, before I knew I wanted to marry Pandora, my stepdad gave me some great advice."

"Lay it on me."

"You know when you know."

That's it? "Care to elaborate?"

"Nothing more to say." Something howled. Mason couldn't be sure whether it was a dog or kid. "Sorry, man, but Pandora's out shopping with a friend and I've got a situation. Seriously, think about what I told you. Best thing

I ever did was trust myself enough to believe in what I was doing."

Mason disconnected and contemplated throwing his phone.

Clearly, his usually logical friend had been brainwashed by love. Nothing he'd just said made sense. Mason had entered his marriage planning to be with the same woman for the rest of his life, but now that the illusion of a *forever* relationship had been shattered, he recognized love for the sham it was.

Sure, he loved his dad, but that was different. No one else could ever have that kind of permanent connection. Melissa proved it wasn't possible.

As for what he felt for Hattie? Mason didn't have a clue.

WITH CHRISTMAS ONLY three weeks away, a sense of urgency had settled over Hattie, driving her to make every minute of each day count. Thanksgiving might've been a bust—at least where her parents were concerned, but no matter what, she was determined to make Santa's big day extra special.

The holiday was always a big deal in Conifer. With a limited amount of decorative items shipped in, homeowners had to be quick in buying items the second they hit Shamrock's or the grocery store.

Tuesday morning, she and Mason loaded the girls into Melissa's SUV to go to a Christmas-tree farm. Hattie had her heart set on the biggest tree she could find.

"You sure we're on the right road?" Mason drove, while both babies gurgled and babbled along to *Elmo's Sing-a-Long*. "And could you please find a different CD?"

"The map said Owl Creek Road. That's what we're on, right?"

Braking, he lowered his mirrored sunglasses to give her

a dark stare. "We're on Deer Creek Road because that's what you told me we needed."

"Oops." She hoped her smile encouraged Mr. Grinch to better appreciate the importance of their mission. This would be the girls' first Christmas, and as such, Hattie thought it important to do everything perfect—just the way her sister would've. Hattie had always wanted to visit the farm, but her parents put up an artificial tree. "You have to admit that with all the snow piled on the shoulders, it looks the same?"

"Sure. Except for the sign that says Owl Creek Road."

"Sorry. Once we get there, you'll be superhappy we drove all this way. Clementine got her tree here last year and it was gorgeous."

He shook his head.

Thirty minutes later, they finally reached Olde St. Nick's Tree Farm. On a weekday, the train wasn't running, but there were plenty of trees and a black pony named Coal for the girls to ride. The building that housed Santa, as well as hot chocolate and cookies, had been decorated to resemble a Dickensian village. Thousands of lights twinkled from most every surface, lighting the suddenly cloudy day. With carols playing over loudspeakers and scents of cinnamon and pine lacing the air, Hattie couldn't imagine a better place for Mason to finally find his holiday spirit.

The place was so popular, families from neighboring towns rode the ferry to catch the farm's specially outfitted retired school bus that hauled trees on top. Since it was open only two weeks out of the year, customers had to be on their game to make sure they were there in time to make the best selection.

"Isn't this adorable?" Hattie asked Mason as they left the car, each carrying a girl. "Should we take pictures of the twins riding the pony first, or visiting Santa?"

"I thought we were here to get a tree? Should be an in-and-out mission. Precision all the way."

"What is it with you and missions? This will be Van's and Viv's first time to see the big guy. I want to soak it in."

He locked the car. "Thought you were asking your mom to come with you?"

"I did, but as usual, she turned me down."

"Sorry."

"It is what it is," Hattie said in a forced cheery tone. She was tired of feeling hurt by her mom. In the same respect, she refused to give up on making their relationship as special as it had once been.

"What happened to the sun?" He tucked his sunglasses into his coat pocket. "I thought it wasn't supposed to snow till tonight?"

"I say bring it on. It'll create an even more festive mood."

"You do know you sound like a lunatic elf, right? From all I've read, I doubt the girls will even remember this Christmas."

"But they'll have pictures. Do you want them being the only kids at school who didn't meet with Santa?"

"News flash—" he opened the gate to the pony corral "—they've got a while till kindergarten."

"Just hush."

Since the lot was nearly empty, Coal's wrangler gave the twins an extralong ride. While Mason walked alongside the pony, holding both girls in the same saddle, Hattie took pictures with her phone, trying not to think how lucky Vanessa and Vivian were to be held by such a handsome guy.

A few minutes in, the pony snorted. Vivian got spooked and launched into an instant wail.

"That's it." Mason plucked both girls from the saddle. "Ride's over. Let's grab the tree before snow sets in."

"Nope," she said. "Santa's next."

While the quintessential Kris Kringle jiggled the now-smiley twins, Hattie snapped more shots. "Aren't they the cutest things you've ever seen?"

"Ho, ho, ho," Santa said. "I'll bet you two want some pretty new rattles for Christmas." His boisterous laugh terrified Vanessa.

Mason was first to snatch Vanessa and Vivian back into his arms. "Now that both babies have been thoroughly traumatized, can we get on with this?"

"What's up with you?" she asked out of earshot of Mrs. Claus, who'd handed them all candy canes.

"This just isn't my thing, okay?"

"What do you mean?" She took Vanessa from him.

"The over-the-top holiday scene."

"I never knew you didn't like Christmas." She glanced his way to find his profile darker than the approaching storm clouds.

"I don't have anything personal against it." He stepped over an extension cord, then extended his hand to steady her. "But Mom died the week before, so ever since, that memory overrides anything else."

"Please don't think I'm being flippant, but have you ever thought about making new memories? You spent lots of holidays with us and seemed happy enough."

He snorted. "That's because Melissa was always nagging me to smile."

"I'm sorry." And she really was. All too clearly she recalled the sad little boy he'd long ago been. It hurt her that he still missed his mom. It also made her all the more determined to help heal her own mother's emotional pain.

After interlocking her fingers with his, she squeezed.

"See any of these you like?" They'd reached the portion of the lot where precut trees stood in neat rows.

"Nice stab at changing the subject." Standing on her tip-toes, she kissed him. "What if this Christmas you remember the happy times with your mom? Even better, what if I make this holiday so perfect you can't wait to have dozens more just like it?"

Groaning, he drew her into a hug. "You're too good to be true. I don't deserve you."

"No, you don't," she teased, "but for now, anyway, I'm here and you're here and the most adorable baby angels are here. What if we make believe we're a real family?"

"That what you want to do?"

She swallowed hard. Hattie didn't know what she wanted beyond being with this man, which went against everything she knew to be true. If he played along with her silly game, it'd be just that—a game. After New Year's, he'd be gone, just like the season. But it wouldn't even be like a legitimate breakup because how could she claim a man who'd never really been hers, but her sister's?

Making matters worse, as was usually the case in their small town, their hug had been witnessed. Her opinionated regular from the bar, Rufus, had apparently secured seasonal work at the farm and stood a few yards away, trimming a tree bottom—and wagging his finger in her direction.

Chapter Fifteen

Back from the tree farm, Mason unearthed Melissa's tree stand from the downstairs storage area, hauled it upstairs, then crammed the odd little tree they'd purchased into it. "Want me to pile a few books under it so it looks taller?"

Hattie held Vanessa on her hip while appraising the partially bald tree. "It seemed bigger outside."

She'd gotten her dates mixed up and missed the farm's famed opening weekend. It was then, the salesman had explained, that the best trees were sold. All of the majestic ones Hattie had set her heart upon regally standing in the cathedral-like living room had already been sold. The tree they'd bought was cute—if a little lopsided—but barely stood five feet tall.

Vivian honked the horn on her new walker toy.

Mason chuckled. "Viv seems to like it, so it can't be all that bad."

"Yeah, but I wanted a perfect tree. You know how Melissa always wanted even her old bedroom to look like it was out of a magazine. How could I have gotten the tree farm's opening dates so wrong?"

"Gee, could it be you lost your sister, your mom and dad dived off the deep end, you broke your arm and suddenly are the primary caregiver to not one baby, but two?"

She sat on the sofa arm. "When you put it that way, guess I have had a lot on my mind."

"You think?" He went to her, enfolding her in his arms. "Tell you what, tomorrow morning, if you still find this tree lacking, let's go out and cut our own."

"Really?"

"Have you looked outside? This land is covered in Christmas trees. How hard can it be to chop one down?"

HATTIE WOKE SPOONED alongside Mason the next morning. Though the clock read 6:00 a.m., it was still dark and would be for a while. He'd molded his fingers to the curve of her stomach. She placed her hand over his, toying with the fine hair on his knuckles.

"You're up too early," he said with a sexy growl, burrowing beneath her hair to kiss her neck. "If we're lucky, the munchkins will snooze for at least another thirty minutes."

"I'm up because I'm excited."

"Yeah? Me, too…." His claim was confirmed by the size of his erection. "What are we going to do about all this excitement?"

"I thought we were headed into the woods to find a giant Christmas tree?"

He rolled her over for a long, leisurely kiss that tugged an invisible string of arousal. "Wouldn't you rather stay in bed?"

She giggled when he nibbled her ear. "I suppose we could, but then what are we going to do about getting a bigger tree?"

"Oh—something's getting bigger as we speak."

"You're awful!"

"You're delicious," he said after another heated kiss.

"Let's get this show on the road before our two monkeys start rattling around in their cages."

Hours later, once the sun finally rose on twelve inches of freshly fallen snow, they bundled the girls for their trek out onto the twenty acres of forest on which the house sat.

"You do know this is crazy, right?" The sight of him took her breath away. The way cold turned his cheeks ruddy and his winter coat accentuated his size. Even when she'd been little, he'd made her feel safe—like anything was possible.

"This coming from the guy who took all the desks from the school to spell out your class year on the football field?"

"Child's play." He took one step outside of the circle drive the local plowing service had cleared and stood in snow up to his thighs. "Got any ideas on how to carry the chain saw and two babies through this?"

"You're the SEAL."

"Really? Is that how this is going to be?" The way the corners of his eyes crinkled when he smiled made her want him all over again.

"You started it. Just be glad I can't hold Vanessa and make a snowball at the same time, or you'd be pummeled."

"Like this?" Before she could even form a plan for making a one-armed snowball, he'd already succeeded, lobbing it straight at her head.

"Beast!" The shocking cold of snow against every inch of her face had her laughing, but seeking revenge. A chase ensued. "I hate you!"

"No, you don't," he teased, always an infuriating few steps ahead.

When he finally slowed enough for her to nail his bare neck with a handful of lightly packed snow, he growled upon impact, landing her and Vanessa in a playful tackle against mounded snow.

Breathing heavy and smiling, she said, "You're horrible, attacking poor defenseless girls like that."

"Aw, I'm not so bad." The sizzling heat of his slow, sexy grin did crazy, happy things to her chest. Sheer anticipation of wanting his kiss made it impossible to breathe. Consulting Vivian, he asked, "You think I'm fun, don't you?"

The infant gave him a toothless grin.

"See? All the ladies love me." He leaned in close enough for his warm breath to tickle Hattie's upper lip.

Yes, Mason, you would be so easy to love.

In an attempt to steer the conversation away from her heart, she asked, "How is any of this helping me get a bigger Christmas tree?"

He laughed, then kissed her. "As seems to be a trend when I'm around you, something's getting bigger."

"You're horrible!" And so ridiculously sexy she could happily occupy this spot for hours.

"Admit it, you can't get enough of me…." He kissed her again and again, and as much as she wanted to deny him, she lacked the strength. Like a chip or cookie, when it came to his kisses she had to have one more.

"Okay, yes, I'm hopelessly addicted to you, so will you now get my tree?"

"Have you always been this demanding?"

She raised her chin and smiled. "Yes. So kiss me one last time and then get moving. Since the snow's deeper than we thought, the girls and I will stay here."

"Deal."

Only after Hattie and the girls waved Mason on his way, she found herself craving still more…

MASON COULDN'T HAVE said why, but his mission to find Hattie her quintessential Christmas tree had taken on an absurd sense of urgency. Above all else, he wanted to see her smile—better yet, be the one responsible for producing that smile.

He trudged at least a half mile through thigh-deep snow before discovering a twelve-footer that even Hattie would be hard-pressed to deny was impressive. Not too wide and perfectly symmetrical, it was a true beauty—just like the woman he'd be bringing it home for.

While priming the finicky chain saw, it occurred to Mason that over the past few weeks—especially since sleeping in a real bed next to Hattie—Melissa and Alec's house had started feeling more like a home. But what did that mean? Was it the actual house he felt comfortable with, or the occupants? All it took was remembering that morning's kisses and the twins' adorably goofy grins to tell him without a doubt, the ladies of the house had placed a spell over him.

Weeks earlier, he'd found himself living for the navy. It spooked him how suddenly new commitments had taken precedence.

But was he honestly committed to Hattie and the twins? Or had he succumbed to the privileges of playing house with benefits?

Frustrated with this train of thought, he used a collapsible shovel he'd stashed in a backpack to dig out around the tree's base—no easy feat as beneath the snow, it'd been broader than he'd anticipated.

No worries, though. He'd told Hattie he'd bring her a tree and by God, that was what he'd do.

His next course of action was to start the small chain saw he'd also hauled along. He yanked repeatedly at the saw's pull start, only nothing happened. Even as a kid he'd had a hatred for two-cycle engines. Apparently, they hated him back.

He tugged and tugged, primed and primed, until finally giving up and opting for an old scout hatchet he'd brought for backup.

With the sky darkening and the temperature dropping, he figured he'd better put his back into it or he'd be there all night.

When he'd been a full-time Alaskan, he'd been a fisherman—not a woodsman—so his ax man skills left a lot to be desired. He knew enough to make a V in the trunk, but best as he could remember, the placement of that V was critical as to which direction the tree would fall.

Hoping for the best, Mason made a judgment call when giving the larger-than-expected tree a final shove. Wood cracked, and with a mighty whoosh the tree was down.

Now he just had to drag it home…

TWO HOURS PASSED. When Mason still hadn't returned to the house, worry set in. The man was a navy SEAL. No doubt he could single-handedly take down a grizzly, then roast him for dinner, but Alaska was loaded with manly men and sadly, they died all the time.

Though Hattie's more rational side knew he was most likely fine, the part of her still shocked by the sudden loss of her sister and brother-in-law warned her not to take chances. After all of their horseplay, it'd been noon before he'd set off. This time of year, especially with cloud cover, they had barely two hours of daylight left—if that.

Pacing the kitchen, she dialed her parents' number, praying at least her father would recognize the potential urgency of the situation. "Dad, I'm sorry to bother you," she said once he picked up, "but I need your help. I'm afraid Mason may be in trouble."

"Be right there" was all he said before hanging up.

Snow was really coming down, along with the temperature, so Hattie popped the girls in their playpen, then took their monitor outside.

"Mason!" Falling snow combined with wind in the pines deadened the sound of her voice. "Mason, can you hear me?"

No response.

If something had happened to him all because she'd sent him out to look for a stupid Christmas tree, she'd never forgive herself.

Shivering with no coat, she dashed back inside.

Kneeling alongside the playpen, willing her pulse to slow, she said to the girls, "Right about now I'm wishing you guys were old enough to talk to. Better yet, that you were old enough to talk some sense into me about not needing everything to be perfect—especially not decorations."

When Melissa had been alive, she'd gladly assumed the role of family Martha Stewart, but that had never been Hattie's thing. Why now did she feel compelled to try to re-create things the way Melissa had done them? Could it be linked to her insecurities about Mason? How she still didn't completely believe he was as into her as she was him?

The doorbell rang, and Hattie rushed to answer.

Her dad was an avid backcountry snowshoer. Many times they'd gone together, and he carried her snowshoes with him.

"Thank you so much for coming." She crushed him in a hug.

"We'll find him. His tracks should be easy enough to follow."

"But I can't leave the babies."

"I'll watch them." Her mom's movements were sluggish, her expression grim, but she was really there, holding out her arms for a hug.

Hattie asked, "Are you sure you'll be okay?"

She nodded. "I'll be fine. We'll talk later, but for now, you two go on and bring Mason safely home."

Her dad was right in that, even with worsening weather, Mason's trail was clear. Seeing how deeply he'd sunk into the snow made her nauseous. Why had she insisted he do it?

The deeper into the forest they trekked, the harder snow fell and the darker the skies grew.

Hattie's chest tightened to the point she feared having some sort of attack. "Mason!"

"Maaason!" her father echoed. To her he asked, "How're you doing with your bum arm?"

"I'm fine. It's Mason I'm worried about."

"We'll find him. I told your mom that if we're not back in an hour, she should call for backup."

A few more steps later, Hattie was almost afraid to ask, "How'd you get Mom to come?"

"I didn't. She's got herself down to taking those tranquilizers only at night. She wanted to be here."

"Th-that's great," Hattie said. Her teeth started to chatter, only not from cold, but concern for Mason. Another new item on her list of issues was that if her mom was doing better, why hadn't she called? Was she still upset over the will?

"Mason!" her dad called.

"Lyle?" answered a voice from out of the dark. Then came an odd swishing sound.

"Mason! Thank God." When he came into view, tears fell fast and hard. As best she could in her awkward snowshoes, Hattie went to him, tossing her arms around his neck, kissing him full on his lips, not caring who saw. "I've been so scared something happened. What took you so long?"

After returning her kiss, he drew her attention to a hulking form behind him. "What do you think took so long? Your tree. In case you haven't noticed, it's a monster."

Lyle asked, "Why'd you pick one so big?"

Mason laughed. "Your daughter wanted one this size. I was afraid if I brought anything smaller, she wouldn't let me in the house. The only thing keeping me going was my fantasy of returning to a steaming spiked coffee."

Now quaking with gratitude for Mason being all right, Hattie shook her head. "You stupid, silly man. I would have promised you a lifetime supply of spiked coffee if you'd come home an hour ago."

"I'd have taken you up on that," he said with a sexy wink barely visible from the light of her dad's head lamp, "but I didn't dare come home without this tree."

"YOU'RE SAFE." Mason was shocked when Akna opened the front door for him, then made the sign of the cross on her chest.

"Sorry for giving you all a fright." He was too cold to put much thought into the implications of his ex-mother-in-law's appearance. For Hattie's sake, he hoped this meant a return to the closeness she and her mom had once shared. "This whole Christmas-tree thing has gotten out of hand."

When he'd voiced his complaint in Hattie's direction, she'd at least had the good graces to redden, but then he found genuine regret behind her half smile and was sorry for his continued teasing. "I never should've asked you."

"Now that the tree's down," Lyle said, "we might as well put it up. Your sister likes her tree in the front window, right, Hattie?"

Hugging the coat she'd only just removed, she nodded. "I'll get the little tree out of the stand."

Outside with Lyle, Mason tried and failed again to get

the chain saw working so he could trim the trunk and bottom branches.

Lyle asked, "Mind if I take a turn?"

"Be my guest." Mason stepped aside.

Just his luck the stupid thing started right up, making him feel like a gangly twelve-year-old in front of the man whom he'd once held in high regard.

The chain saw's buzz and smoke polluted the calm night.

But after a few minutes' cutting and shaping, Lyle was done. "That should do it."

"Looks good." More than ready to get this chore finished, Mason grabbed the tree by the trunk's base to haul it inside.

"Hold up." Lyle blocked the porch stairs. "While I've got you alone, mind explaining that kiss?"

Chapter Sixteen

"Let me help." When her mother got up from the sofa, Hattie had a hard time even recognizing her. She'd lost a frightening amount of weight and dark shadows haunted her eyes.

"I've got it, Mom. You rest."

"I—I've done enough resting." Hugging herself, she stared at her reflection in the window's glass. "Despite my issues with Mason, I'm glad he wasn't hurt. Even the possibility of another accident was the wake-up call I needed. It's good being back with the girls."

Almost as if they sensed the dark mood, Vanessa and Vivian sat quietly in their walkers. Vanessa gummed a stuffed frog and Vivian stared daggers at a potted fern.

"Mom…" Their family had never been overly demonstrative, which made her mother's admission all the more meaningful, yet hard to hear. Hattie hadn't expected a grand statement, just for her mother to remember the family she still had who loved her so very much. "It's okay."

"I know, but let me get this out. I'll always believe what your sister did—signing her children over to you and a man who should've been out of all of our lives—was an awful betrayal. Then, instead of accepting her wishes like the honor they were, he just—just threw his parental rights away? H-he's awful. Worse."

When Akna started to weep, Hattie wrapped her arms around her mother's frail form. "What he did, it wasn't like that. Mason's a good man, Mom, but he has an important job to get back to. He's not ready to be a parent right now."

"Raising your sister's children isn't important?"

Hattie sighed. "That's not what I meant. It's complicated." If her mom knew exactly how complicated, she'd no doubt ground her.

"Sir?" The kiss question had Mason clearing his throat. "I'm, ah, not sure what you mean."

"Then I'll be blunt." Lyle fit the chain saw back in its plastic case. "Hattie might be all grown up, but as far as I'm concerned, you've already hurt one of my daughters. If your plan is to create that kind of pain all over again, then—"

"Sir..." Mason clenched and unclenched his fists. "I mean no disrespect by this, but Melissa cheated on me. You're a man, so I assume you know what it means to support your family. If I'd been able to stay home every day with Mel, holding her hand every second after that miscarriage, don't you think I would've? Unfortunately, as the man of the house, I didn't have that luxury. To afford your daughter the kind of lifestyle she deserved, I had to work. Fishing was all I'd ever known."

A nerve twitched in Lyle's jaw. "I understand that, but make no mistake, if you're putting the moves on my Hattie, I will do everything within my power to stop you."

Seriously? "What don't you get about the fact that your daughter left me—to be with my best friend. She wasn't the one forced to join the navy, because everywhere I went in this stupid town, all my so-called friends stared at me with pity. Hattie gets me. She's a beautiful, loving woman fully capable of—"

Lyle's hard right to Mason's jaw rendered him momentarily speechless.

It took every shred of Mason's self-restraint not to meet the older man's punch with one of his own. But what would that prove? "Because you're no doubt still grieving, I'll give you a pass for that. What I won't do is accept blame for your eldest daughter making the conscious decision to break her marital vows. As for Hattie, I'm pretty sure she's old enough to make her own decisions."

His ex-father-in-law exhaled with a grunt of what Mason could only describe as disgust, then mounted the porch stairs. "We'll see about that."

"He hit you?" Hattie had just made the girls' dinner bottles and fixed them bowls of peaches when her father stormed into the house, telling her mother it was time for them to leave.

As suddenly as her parents had appeared, they were now gone.

"Yep." Mason fished in the freezer, eventually pulling out a bag of peas he held to his bruising jaw.

Instantly at his side, she asked, "What'd you do?"

His narrow-eyed stare told her she'd asked the wrong question.

"What is it with your family always assuming I'm the one in the wrong? Your old man wanted to know why I kissed you. He then declared you off-limits as far as I was concerned."

Covering her face with her hands, Hattie groaned. "You've got to be kidding."

"Wish I were."

"Now what?" Hattie held Vivian's spoon to her mouth.

"You're asking me?" He did the same for Vanessa.

"Clearly, both of my parents have lost their minds."

Vivian winced, then grinned at her first taste of peaches. "I don't get how they'd rather complain about you than be here with these two cuties."

"Good question." He used a damp washcloth to clean Vanessa's sticky cheeks.

"I'm sorry."

"For what? You didn't hit me."

"Yeah, but if it hadn't been for my stupid Christmas tree, none of this would've happened."

"Speaking of which, it's still out in the front yard. Once we get these two fed, wanna help me bring it in?"

She leaned in to kiss him. "There's nothing I'd rather do."

"Nothing?" He grinned, then winced, reaching for his bag of peas to hold against his jaw. "At the very least, after getting punched out by your dad, you owe me a rousing game of helpless patient/naughty nurse."

HATTIE FINISHED WITH the last of the blue Christmas lights she hung at the bar every year, then climbed down from the stepladder to admire her handiwork.

"Needs to go a good three inches to the right," said Rufus.

"Ignore him," Clementine said from the garnish station. "It looks good." She'd eaten about twenty cherries in the past thirty minutes, but in the holiday spirit of giving, Hattie pretended not to notice. "But I still don't understand how your dad punched out your boyfriend and the very next day you're back at work, decorating up a storm, acting as if nothing happened."

"I'd hardly call Mason my boyfriend."

"Then what would you call him?" She unloaded the silver metallic tree that occupied a place of honor at the base of the stairs.

"Does there have to be a label?"

"I don't suppose, but have you all talked about what happens when he leaves?"

"No." Hattie preferred not thinking about it.

The bar's door opened. Stepping inside on a gust of cold wind was Hattie's father.

Leaving Clementine to deal with the tree's many parts, Hattie met him before he selected a seat. "You hit him? Dad, that's not you." When her voice cracked, she swallowed hard. "You've always been one of the kindest, gentlest men I know. What's happening to not only you, but our family?"

"It's complicated." He removed his Conifer Cardinals ball cap. "All I know is Mason destroyed Melissa and he'll do the same to you. He's not cut out to be a family man—never has been, never will."

"Are you delusional?" When her raised voice drew stares from the customers seated at the bar, she tugged her father by his sleeve to a lonely row of booths. "You and Mom never wanted to accept the fact that your supposedly perfect daughter cheated on her husband, but she did. I'm sorry she'd had a miscarriage, but that never justified her sleeping around with Alec—her husband's best friend. Why can't you see that? Moreover, why can't you recognize Mason as the injured party in that whole mess? Melissa and Alec kept all their mutual friends. Mason didn't just lose his wife, but his entire world."

Her dad slowly exhaled. "Can you grab me a beer?"

"No. Not until you admit you were wrong to hit Mason and owe him an apology, but also that I deserve some happiness. If Mason makes me smile, then how can that be wrong?"

"Fine. You won't give me a beer, I'll take my business elsewhere."

"You're impossible," she called after her father when he slapped his hat back on and headed for the door.

"And you're delusional. Mark my words, that boy will bring you nothing but pain."

"He's not a boy, but a man," she whispered once her dad was gone. "And at the moment, I respect him more than you."

Rufus shook his head. "You shouldn't disrespect your father like that."

"Yeah? Well, thanks for the advice, but I'm damned sick and tired of him disrespecting *me*."

"REMIND ME WHY we're standing in line for the girls to see Santa for the second time this year?" The Saturday before Christmas, Mason pushed their stroller ahead by a measly foot down the North Pole Trail that was actually the longest stretch of Conifer's wharf that didn't have any businesses built off of it. Fresh pine garland had been hung from the railings and the choir from Eastside Church sang carols. Food stands sold funnel cake, cider and cocoa.

Even the weather was being cooperative, with plenty of sun and no wind.

He'd been to Conifer's annual Christmas parade and festival every year of his life until leaving for the navy. So why did it feel as if he'd landed on the moon without a space suit?

"Why wouldn't we bring them to see Santa? You saw him here when you were a kid, right?" She tucked Vivian's blanket more snugly around her shoulders.

"Sure. We all did, but I'm just saying the girls could get confused by the concept of multiple Santas, since they just met him at the tree lot."

"Whatever. Just stand there and look handsome."

Had they been alone, he'd have landed a light smack to

her behind for being sassy. Unfortunately, they were surrounded by couples he and Melissa had graduated with. His skin crawled from the weight of their stares.

"What's wrong?" Hattie asked. "You're glowering as if someone stole your candy cane."

"I just hate how everyone's staring."

"Who?" She glanced around.

"I don't know. Just everyone."

"Since when did you become self-conscious? And for the record, I'm pretty sure Jingles the Elf Clown is drawing way more of a crowd than you."

They moved forward another couple feet. "Forget I said anything, okay? Let's just get this over with and head back to the house."

"Don't you want to go to the craft sale? For all they've done to help with the girls, I want to find something special for your dad and Fern."

"Please, Hattie, can we just—"

"Hey, Mason. Long time no see." Craig Lovett, the guy from Mason's senior class who'd had his birthday party at Alec and Melissa's that fateful last night, held out his hand for Mason to shake. "I'm in awe of you, man. You're an honest-to-God SEAL. You're living the dream."

His wife, Sue, who manned their stroller, tugged a lock of Craig's hair. "I thought *we* were *the dream?*"

Craig backpedaled by giving his wife a quick kiss. "Honey, you know what I mean. What guy wouldn't want to be a SEAL? I always planned to be one, but never found time. Is it true that during Hell Week you have to kill a shark with your bare hands?"

"Nah." Where did guys get this stuff? Craig had been such a jackass to him during the divorce that Mason was sorely tempted to yank his chain by claiming they had to kill not just *any* shark, but a great white. Instead, as he'd been trained, he took the high road. "No sharks, just plenty of running and heavy lifting."

"Oh." Craig's shoulders deflated. "Well, you did have to stay underwater for twenty-four hours while breathing through a reed, right? I'd have nailed that."

Mason slowly dragged down his sunglasses. "Underwater breathing techniques are top secret, man. If I told you about them, I'd have to kill you."

"Sure. I get it. Whoa." He shook his head. "That's hardcore, but I could handle it. Maybe I should look into enlisting?"

Sue rolled her eyes before asking Hattie, "How are the twins? Losing both their parents had to be rough. Our oldest son, Frank, lost his hamster when he was two. I thought he'd need therapy to stop crying."

"Um, yeah." Mason couldn't be sure, but he'd have sworn Hattie glanced his way for help. If he'd read her right, she wanted to escape this couple as badly as he did. To Mason, she said, "I just remembered we were supposed to pick up those cookies I ordered at two and the bakery closes in ten minutes. We've got to go."

"Oh, gosh—" Sue scooted their youngest child's stroller aside when Hattie almost ran her down with the twins. "Well, it was nice seeing you."

"Mason," Craig called, "when you get a chance, stop by the store. I'd love hearing your battle stories."

"Will do," Mason said with a backhand wave.

Safely out of earshot, Hattie slowed to her more normal sedate pace. "Can you believe the nerve of that woman? Comparing Viv and Van's loss to losing a hamster? And did you really have to breathe through a reed for twenty-four hours?"

"What do you think?"

She laughed. "No, but considering you just chopped a

giant tree, then dragged it back to the house and single-handedly crammed that sucker into a stand, at this point I'd pretty much believe anything about you."

"Why do you stick around here?"

She crossed the street that had been closed for the day to only foot traffic. "What do you mean?"

"Please don't take this the wrong way, but I don't remember high school being a particularly good time for you. Why do you hang around with people like that?"

"I don't. They were my sister's friends—used to be yours."

He winced. "Don't remind me. I've changed. They seem as self-involved as ever."

"I love Conifer. There's my family and the bar. Great friends like Clementine and all my regulars. There's low crime and lots of fun things to do. I can't imagine a better place to raise a family—especially now that I just happen to have one."

"I admire you." He opened the door to the rec hall, where the craft fair was being held. "Don't think I could do it."

"Did anyone ask you to?" Her snarky tone alerted him to the question's layers. What did she really want to know? Whether or not he was asking if she'd ever consider leaving Conifer? Or if he'd ever consider staying?

HATTIE MIGHT OUTWARDLY be humming along to "Silent Night" as she and Mason browsed the craft-fair items, but that didn't mean she was calm.

Before breaking her arm, she'd had a handle on the situation with Mason. She'd known exactly where she stood with him. They'd shared the blizzard party, and after that, had she not been stupid enough to trip down those stairs, he'd have been long gone. Since then, no matter how hard she'd tried convincing herself she wasn't attracted to him, and that she didn't even want him because he'd been Melissa's first, Hattie was beginning to fear her efforts futile.

Who was she kidding? Mason had always been a part of her, but that didn't mean squat when it came to him making a meaningful commitment to her.

His charging to her rescue now was no different from when he'd carried her home after the sledding accident that had broken her ankle. He cared, but that was all. By his own admission, after what her sister had done to him, he was incapable of giving more.

Which was why she had to stop viewing him as the handsome man of her dreams and start seeing him for what he was—her sister's bitter ex. No more swooning over his ridiculous body and looks. It was time to be adult about the situation and stop acting like a love-sick preteen.

"Think Fern might like this?" With a goofy, game show–model flourish, he held up a house-shaped tissue-box cover. The tissue came out of the house's chimney. It was so well made, yet so kitschy, Hattie loved it and his over-the-top presentation.

"I bet she will." How did he do it? Just when she vowed to cure herself of her unhealthy Mason addiction, he went and did something adorable to drag her back in.

THIRTY MINUTES LATER, Hattie stood alongside Mason in Craig's sporting-goods store while he surveyed fishing poles.

"Dad's been bitching for years about losing his best rod steelhead fishing on the Situk River. About time he got back out there."

While Mason took forever selecting just the right one, Hattie remembered all the times she'd shopped here with Melissa and her mom for her dad. Father's Day and his birthday and Christmas, the three of them had been here, debating over whether to get fishing tackle or hunting gear. Back then, she never would have guessed how distant she and her family would now be.

Her parents would no doubt place all the blame for their current state of affairs on Mason, but they'd be wrong. The man and woman she'd once believed infallible were human just like everyone else.

She wasn't sure whether to be happy or sad about that fact. On the one hand, it came as somewhat of a relief to know her parents were mortal. On the flip side, why had they chosen now to fall apart? Yes, Melissa had died, and because of that, part of their family was gone forever, but for her, for their grandchildren, they couldn't fall apart. More than ever, she needed them, but after her dad hit Mason, what would she even say?

Going to see them before her father apologized would make her feel traitorous.

"I think this one." Mason plucked a rod from the rack. "Dad will love it. What're you getting your dad?"

"A sack of coal. I'm still furious with him. Aren't you?"

While Hattie pushed the stroller, they headed toward the checkout. "At first, yeah, I was plenty pissed, but then I put myself in his shoes. He lost his daughter, and that loss doesn't make sense. One minute she was in his life, the next she was gone, so he's striking out. I just happened to be there."

They were next in line, which squelched the conversation—probably a good thing, as she'd need a moment to process Mason's charitable take on the situation. She waited until they were in the car to ask, "How can you be so forgiving toward my dad?"

Mason backed out of their parking space. "How should I act? Lyle used to be like my second father. I thought the world of him. His punch didn't hurt so much physically, as emotionally. I don't understand, though, how they still view the divorce as such a black-and-white issue, with me one hundred percent at fault."

"I've never gotten it, either." Out on the main roads, traffic was a nightmare. The pretty day this close to Christmas was such a rarity that it seemed the whole town had come out to celebrate. "But I'm sure Melissa's bad-mouthing didn't help."

The moment Hattie mentioned her sister's bad sportsmanship regarding the divorce, guilt consumed her. Especially with Melissa gone, she shouldn't have been disloyal to the sister she'd loved.

But then, what did she owe Mason? In such a short time, he'd come to mean so much, which frightened her. From the start, what they'd shared was never supposed to be more than a temporary good time. A way to feel better when nothing in her life felt right.

At the next stoplight, Mason asked, "Melissa trashtalked me a lot to your folks?"

"I—I suppose." She tried looking down, but he placed his fingers beneath her chin, urging her to meet his gaze.

"What exactly did she say?"

"I don't want to do this. It doesn't feel right."

"Oh—but your sister making false claims about me to your parents was?"

"I didn't mean that."

They finally broke free of traffic, but for the next few miles, and then hours, Mason didn't speak a word.

Chapter Seventeen

That night, Mason stood in front of the twelve-foot tree he'd lugged from the forest to help Hattie decorate. They'd draped it in lights—the last available from both Shamrock's and the grocery store. They'd hung all of Melissa and Alec's ornaments—some Mason even remembered having been around back when they'd been married. So here it sat, this monument to the holiday, but what had it solved or proved?

Hattie's relationship with her parents was worse than ever. Melissa's perfect house had been maintained, but what did it matter if no one saw it but him and Hattie? The twins were supposed to be having a magical first Christmas, but as long as they had plenty of bottles, clean diapers and hugs, he got the impression they couldn't care less about the season's opulent trappings Hattie insisted they have.

So, in the end, after all of this work, what had he and Hattie accomplished? Part of him felt rather than celebrating the true meaning of Christmas, all they had done was construct an elaborate altar at which they were supposed to worship Melissa's memory. Only that wasn't what he'd signed up to do.

Come to think of it, what *was* he doing? It'd taken Hattie a couple days to get past the initial shock of her broken arm, but since then, her cast hadn't slowed her. So if she didn't need him, why hadn't he gone back to base? Why had he stayed in Conifer, playing house, when he could be making a genuine difference for his country?

"You ever speaking to me again?" Hattie had been downstairs, folding laundry. He'd offered to do it for her, but in typical Hattie fashion, she'd refused.

He shrugged.

Stepping up behind him, she slipped her hands around his waist, resting her head between his shoulder blades. "I am sorry. Before Melissa died, I one hundred percent took your side in the divorce. I still feel the same, but her dying tangled it all up in my mind. My sister never said anything *that* heinous about you—she just excelled at playing the poor, innocent victim. I guess the only way she could reconcile her actions into not being your garden-variety adultery was by claiming you were gone so often that she'd been forced to turn to Alec for support. Total B.S., but there you have it—the world according to Melissa."

Strangely unable to cope with even the few hours' separation their argument had caused, Mason placed his hands over Hattie's. "Thanks. As much as it hurts, now that I know the specifics of what your parents believe I did, that puts me somewhat on an even playing field. Trouble is, with your sister not here to back me up, we both know who they're most likely always going to believe."

"I am sorry...."

Turning to face her, he ran his hands along her upper arms. "Know what's funny?"

Her sad smile filled his heart to near bursting. "I honestly can't think of a single funny thing."

"Okay, so maybe *funny* isn't the right word. More *enlightening,* but the fact is that as long as I have you on my side, I don't care what your parents think."

She had no response.

"Wishing you felt the same?"

Nodding, she crushed him in a hug. "Everything's such a complicated mess. I don't know what to believe."

He kissed the top of her head. "How about we table the topic for now, turn off this obscene amount of lights and focus on what we do best...." Pressing his lips on hers filled him with the same excitement as when he stepped foot on American ground after having been gone on an extended mission. As much as it terrified him to admit it, all the way out here in tiny Conifer, Alaska, with his best childhood friend who'd somehow become more, when he hadn't even been looking, Mason had finally found home.

Only trouble was, how the hell was he going to keep it? More important, considering what an abysmal failure he'd been at family life before, was he 100 percent sure he wanted it?

Two days before Christmas, instead of going to her bar as Hattie told Mason she'd be doing, she stopped by her parents' home. Though Mason teased her about having adopted Melissa's quest for perfection, Hattie took it seriously. As the twins' mom, she had to be as diligent as possible with every aspect of parenting. While she'd never reach Melissa's degree of perfection, she would always try to do her best.

Approaching the front door, she felt her nerves take over.

Her mom usually went all-out with holiday decoration, but the same fall wreath that'd been on the door the day of Melissa's death was still there, droopy and faded and crusty with ice.

Hattie's relationship with her parents had degraded to the point she rang the doorbell instead of walking in.

"What a nice surprise." Of all people, Hattie hadn't expected her mother to answer the door, but she was cautiously optimistic about seeing her mom out of bed. "Did you bring the twins?"

"No." In the entry hall, Hattie slipped her arms from her coat.

"I'm almost afraid to ask who's with them."

This again? "Mason. And he's great, Mom. They adore him."

She sighed. "Come on in. Can I get you anything? Tea?"

"No, thank you." The home Hattie had grown up in had always been cluttered, but clean. Now it just looked sad. Dishes and newspapers littered the counters. The dining room table was piled with photo albums. "Where's Dad?"

"Working late. Keeping busy seems to help him cope."

"What about you? Are you doing anything special for yourself?"

Akna sat on the sofa, then flipped through a pile of photos she'd taken from the side table. "I'm thinking of taking up scrapbooking. It'll be a big project, but you can help. I want to make a special book for each year of your sister's life. Maybe even two or three per year for those times when she was extra busy. I'm seriously debating leaving out her wedding pictures with Mason, though. This project is meant to celebrate her life, so it doesn't seem right to feature a time that caused her such pain."

Hattie had never wanted to bang her head against a wall more than she did now. "Um, please don't take this the wrong way, but why are you and Dad so fixated on blaming Mason for everything bad that ever happened to Mel?"

For a split second, her mother's wide-eyed, gaping expression caused a flicker of guilt. But then a myriad of beautiful memories Mason had shared with their family not just in the past, but recently, emboldened her to forge ahead.

"When I broke my ankle, do you remember who carried me in from the woods? And whenever Mel procrastinated on school projects, who was always there for her to pick up the slack? Who helped with the yard work and gardening, never expecting to be paid in anything but your ham sandwiches or fish stew? Yes, Mel and Mason's divorce was ugly, but why can't you see he never wanted it? He loved her as much as we did—do. She was his life, and she essentially threw him away. How can you blame him when he was the injured party?"

Seeming flustered, Akna dropped her photos and stooped to gather them. "I thought it might be nice for us to share this scrapbooking project, but you're just upsetting me."

"Mom, I *need* you to be upset." Hattie helped clean the mess. "You have to snap out of your grief long enough to recognize Melissa's girls need their grandmother."

"If I believed that, she'd have left them with me, instead of you."

Heels of her hands pressed to her forehead, Hattie realized she might as well have been talking to the raggedy wreath on the front door. "Don't you get it? In leaving her kids to me, Melissa gave you and Dad a tremendous gift. She freed you from the day-to-day drudgery of constant feedings and baths and laundry so you could be their grandmother. She wanted them to grow up viewing you as a person to be loved and cherished and honored—just like Melissa and I did with your parents and Dad's. Why are you denying them that opportunity? What I especially don't understand is why you're blaming Mason for any of what happened."

What had started as her mother's silent tears now turned

messy. "Why do I blame Mason? B-because if they'd never gotten divorced, your sister never would've married Alec, and she never would've been in his p-plane. Please, leave. J-just go…"

Hattie crossed the room to give her mother a hug, and then abided by her wishes. She'd done all she could to repair their relationship. The next move was solidly in her mother's court.

Pressing her hand to the front door, Hattie said, "You're welcome to share Christmas breakfast with us around nine. Fern and Jerry will be there. I've also invited Alec's mom and dad, though I doubt they'll come. It'd be a real shame for you to miss Viv and Van's first Christmas."

WHILE FERN BABYSAT the twins, Mason browsed Shamrock's with his dad, searching for just the right gifts for Hattie, the girls and Fern—the tissue house thingy they'd purchased at the holiday fair seemed more from Hattie than him. "What about a scarf and glove set?"

His dad laughed. "Son, I think you've moved a ways past that."

"How so?"

"Don't you think she's expecting a ring on her finger?"

Damn near choking on his own spit, Mason asked, "Where'd you get that idea?"

"You two are not only shacking up, but share a couple kids. I've seen you with all three of those girls and you look downright smitten. Why not marry Hattie? She's been trailing after you all doe-eyed practically from the day she could walk."

"Oh, come on…" They passed the jewelry department. "Marriage is a step I only intended to take once, and see where that landed me? Besides, you never married again after losing Mom, so why should I?"

Jerry picked up a box of chocolates, bouncing it between his hands. "The key word there is *lost.* What happened to you was different. Never said anything to you, but to me, your Melissa always struck me as a little too big for her britches. Everyone fawned all over her like her poo didn't stink, but by God, what she and Alec did to you did stink—to high heaven. None of that was your fault, so why have you spent so many years blaming yourself when sweet little Hattie's been here all this time, just waiting for you to realize she's the best thing the Beaumont family ever had to offer?"

Head spinning, Mason wasn't sure what to say other than, "Well, that's easy for you to say, but what about you and Fern? Anyone with eyes could see you two are more than just friends."

"Of course we are."

"Then you're finally admitting you feel a little something extra for her?"

"I should hope so, seeing how I married her ten years ago."

"You what?" Mason froze smack-dab in the center of the blender and toaster aisle.

"You heard me. We decided not to make a big deal out of it. I'm allergic to her dogs, and can't stand most of her shows, so she mostly stays up at her place." He winked. "Without fail, though, we never miss conjugal visits at my place every Saturday night."

"How come you never told me?"

Jerry reached for a pig-shaped cutting board. "Don't recall you ever asked."

"WHAT'RE YOU ALL DOING?" Hattie asked Mason upon returning home from her parents' to find him with the girls on their play mat.

"We're trying to say 'cow,' but all I'm hearing are a lot of *goo*s."

After tossing her coat on the back of the sofa, Hattie joined the cozy trio. "You do realize you're months ahead of schedule for their first words?"

"Most babies say their first official words around twelve months, but clearly we're dealing with prodigies, so I'm anticipating words way sooner than that."

"Uh-huh…" She loved the way just being with him and the girls transformed the most mundane activities into pure magic. Tickling Vivian's tummy, she asked, "Okay, gorgeous, out with it. According to Drill Sergeant Mason, you should be speaking in full sentences by Valentine's Day."

Mason's complexion paled.

"You all right?"

He nodded. "It's inconceivable to me that by the time I see these two again, they could be walking and talking."

"I'm surprised that kind of stuff's even on your radar."

"Why?" He rolled onto his side, taking Vanessa along with him. She sat up, reclining against him. She looked so comfortable, so completely at peace, Hattie couldn't bear thinking of how ruined the girls would be when it came time for Mason to go. "I care a lot about these two."

"I know, but once you gave up your rights, I figured it'd be no big deal for you to walk away."

"Me, too…." His normally easygoing smile struck her as hollow. Did he regret relinquishing custody of the girls? But even if he did, how would he raise them when his career dictated a large portion of his time was spent overseas?

She wanted to tell him about what had happened with her mom, but couldn't. As much as she needed to vent, Mason didn't deserve to be dragged into her mom's irrationally cruel coping methods. Hattie had done her best to remind her mother of happier times they'd all shared, but if she wasn't ready to listen, there was little more Hattie could say.

"Your dad and Fern are coming for Christmas, right?"

"Sure. Why wouldn't they? Oh—and before you answer, have I got news for you."

She sat up, perching Vivian on her lap. "Let's hear it."

"Prepare to have your mind blown—my dad and Fern are married."

"What?"

"Dad and I were out shopping this afternoon when he admitted they tied the knot ten years ago."

"That's the craziest thing I've ever heard."

"I thought so, too."

"Why aren't they living together?" He rattled off a long list of reasons that actually sounded level-headed. "Okay, but why the secret? Someone should've at least thrown them a reception."

He smoothed Vanessa's hair. "They didn't want anyone butting into their business. Sound familiar?"

"Maybe a smidge." Laughing, she held her thumb and forefinger barely apart. "But I'm sure my dad will stop by soon to apologize."

"I'm not holding my breath."

CHRISTMAS MORNING, Hattie was first to wake. Usually the girls slept until seven, which gave her a little time to gather her thoughts and drink her first cup of coffee before slipping into mommy mode.

Moving slow as to not wake Mason, she inched from the bed, only to get a fright when he snagged her around her waist. "Where do you think you're going?"

Hands over her mouth, she laughed. "You scared the you-know-what out of me."

"Sorry. My intention was to scare the pants off of you."

"Get your mind out of the gutter." Her halfhearted slug landed on his delicious biceps, which in turn made her appreciate his idea all the more.

"Why? It's much more fun in the gutter."

After he'd thoroughly kissed her, she had to agree.

By the time they shared a shower guaranteed to land them on Santa's naughty list, the girls were up, demanding their breakfast.

Mason offered what had now become their usual routine. "Divide and conquer?"

"Deal."

After feeding the girls, Mason made a fire in the living room hearth.

Hattie turned on the tree lights and set out three platters of cookies she'd made the night before. Since Clementine's mother had gone on a holiday cruise, she would be over for lunch with her boys. Fern and Jerry were stopping by for breakfast and lunch. She didn't dare hope her parents would make an appearance for even one meal, let alone two.

Back upstairs, Hattie fussed with the girls' red-and-green dresses and put Velcro-latch bows in their hair. She added red tights and black patent shoes. For their first Christmas, she hoped Melissa was smiling down upon her adorable brood.

Downstairs again, she asked Mason, "Mind watching the monkeys for a few minutes? I need to get ready."

He gave her a funny look. "What do you mean? You look great."

She set the twins on his lap. "I'm a hot mess. The pictures we take today will be with the girls the rest of their lives. I don't want them ashamed of Aunt Hattie."

Once he'd placed the twins safely in the sofa corner, he tugged her to his lap. "You are amazing. Whether you're wearing sweats and my T-shirt or a ball gown, in my eyes, there's never been a more beautiful woman."

"Don't..." She glanced down at her ragged nails.

"What?" He kissed her just as the sun peeked over Mount Kneely. His warm lips, the scent of the coffee they'd just shared on his breath, raised goose bumps on her forearms and set happy tingles to flight in her belly. How did he do it? Make her feel like the most special woman on earth with a simple kiss? How had her sister ever found him lacking? Skimming his fingertips over her riotous hair, he stared at her with an intensity she found difficult to meet. "Sun's making your skin and hair glow. You're so beautiful."

"Stop..." she whispered when he nuzzled her neck.

Heart racing, she wished she knew whether or not he honestly meant his kind words—or were they just lines he used on all his girls back in Virginia? How was she ever supposed to know?

Chapter Eighteen

"Too bad for me that this time," he said with a final kiss to her nose, "I have to stop because if I don't, we're never going to open presents."

By the time Hattie finished dressing in her favorite plum turtleneck, black slacks and heels, then straightening her hair and applying makeup, she felt armored to resist Mason's most ardent advances.

She was most vulnerable to him when relaxed. When she wasn't thinking rationally, but emotionally. When she stopped focusing on what was best for her and her nieces and succumbed to Mason's heady charm.

At the base of the stairs, she paused a moment to freeze the idyllic image in her head. Mason had turned carols on the stereo and knelt in front of the girls, who shared the sofa.

"Peekaboooo!" he teased over and over to their delighted shrieks. In a perfect world, she'd give anything for him to stay, but perfection didn't exist. Something, whether it was too much salt in her pumpkin pie or her father punching the man of her dreams, would always be bound to go wrong. From here on out, she'd enter any situation expecting the worst, and then, if even the smallest thing went right, she'd be grateful instead of disappointed.

The bottom stair creaked, alerting Mason to her presence. When he wolf-whistled, she blushed. "Damn. You cleaned up nice. Do I need to change?" He wore pajama pants and no shirt. As far as she was concerned, he looked his sexy best.

"You're fine until company comes." *Fine* was an understatement!

"Cool. Now, can we open presents?"

She laughed. "Sure. But you're playing Santa."

HOURS LATER, the living room filled with smiling faces, Mason gazed across a sea of wrapping paper to see Hattie cradling Vivian. She tickled the girl's belly, eliciting a giggly response. In that moment, a fundamental part of him changed. Ever since Melissa had left him, Mason believed himself not only incapable of commitment, but he'd loathed the thought of it. Now? He couldn't fathom being without not only Hattie, but the twins he'd somehow grown to love every bit as if they were his own little girls. It no longer mattered they'd been created from Melissa and Alec's bond. If anything, he loved them all the more because of it, because if Melissa had never left him, Mason might never have realized the truth that had been right there all along—Hattie was the girl for him.

Always had been.

Always would be.

As if they were connected by an invisible string, she looked up. Her sweet, simple blown kiss proved his undoing. The act that finally made him understand the profound piece of advice his friend Calder had shared.

You know when you know.

"MOM! DOUGIE CHEATED!" Clementine's oldest son's booming voice made Hattie wince.

"Did not," three-year-old Dougie proclaimed. They played his new Candy Land game Santa had brought.

Clementine topped her famous candied yams with mini-marshmallows. "Sorry they're so hyper. I warned you that if you craved a nice, peaceful holiday, we were the wrong crew to invite."

Hattie waved off her concern. "They're adorable. And the last thing I want is quiet. It'll only remind me of my parents, who I fear are holed up in their creepy-dark house, dining on TV dinners."

"Thought you'd decided not to worry about them?" Fern noted, checking on the ham she'd brought to their party.

Mason and his dad watched football with the babies on the downstairs TV.

"Easier said than done. I'm frustrated with them, but also worried. What's it going to take for them to come back to the real world?"

"Time." Fern slipped her arm around Hattie's shoulders. "This is probably the last thing you want to hear, but a year or two from now, they'll probably be back to their usual selves, doting on the twins and meddling in your business."

"Oh—they've already got that covered." Clementine tossed the empty marshmallow bag in the recycling bin. "Hattie, did you tell Fern about your dad hitting Mason when he saw him kiss you?"

Hattie shot her friend a dirty look. "I thought we weren't talking about that?"

Fern waved off her concern. "I knew hours after it happened. In the time he's been back, Mason and his dad have grown real close."

Hattie shut her eyes, wishing for so many things she couldn't fit them all into a single prayer. Had her parents not been grief-stricken to the point of insanity—better yet, had Melissa never died—how might things be different?

What if she and Mason had had their reunion by chance, and then romance had blossomed? Would her folks have then embraced their relationship? Would Hattie trust he was attracted to only her, and not the ghost of her sister he may still see in Hattie's eyes or smile?

"WHEW…" MASON CLOSED the door on the last of their guests. "I was beginning to fear they'd never leave."

"Me, too." At ten, the twins had long since been bathed and tucked in by Fern and Jerry, who seemed to enjoy their new role as adoptive grandparents so much that they'd hardly argued at all. As much as she'd enjoyed being around her friends, she'd still sorely missed her family.

In the kitchen, she and Mason worked in tandem to unload the dishwasher.

Nearly finished, she asked, "Am I a bad person for not having taken Van and Viv to see my parents? Was I too harsh, expecting them to come here?"

He snorted. "You're asking me? To my way of thinking your parents and Alec's have a lot of lost time to make up for with their granddaughters, and no one to blame for it but themselves."

Abandoning their task, she hugged him. "In case I haven't told you lately, thank you—for sticking around after I broke my arm, for not returning my dad's punch. Thanks for everything. I'll be so sorry to see you go."

He tensed. "About that… What would you say if I didn't?"

Hands pressed to his chest, she didn't dare hope that was what he meant. His heart beat so hard, she felt its comforting rhythm. "Are you thinking of asking for another extension on your leave?"

"Not exactly." When he dropped to one knee, then took her left hand, her pulse took off on a perilous course. With his free hand, he reached into his back pocket, pulling out a simple, yet lovely diamond solitaire ring. "I found this when I was out shopping with my dad. I want you to marry me, Hat Trick. I'm tired of playing house. Let's do it for real."

Was this a dream? "M-Mason...I don't know what to say."

"I should think it's fairly obvious."

"Yes, but—"

"Then you will? Marry me?"

Yes! her heart screamed.

"I'm sorry, but no," her head forced her to say. How long had she dreamed of a moment like this, yet without all the baggage? With 100 percent trust this was wholly what he wanted—*she* was wholly what he wanted.

"I'm sorry, what?" Brow furrowed, he shook his head. "Did you just turn me down?"

"What did you expect? There's this whole mess with my parents to sort out and the fact that you live about a gazillion miles from here. Not to mention the not-so-little concern that maybe the whole town's right, and I am stepping right into my sister's life. It's all a little too convenient, don't you think?"

His gaze narrowed. "Did you really turn down my proposal because you're on the outs with your parents or afraid of what the town thinks?"

Chin raised, she didn't back down from his angry stare. "Can you blame me for having doubts? Everything between us happened so fast...."

He tossed his hands in the air. "Gee, Hattie, I guess when I asked you to marry me, not because of some sense of duty, but because I thought I loved you, I kind of expected *your* opinion—not your mom's or dad's or Sophie's or that old curmudgeon's who never leaves your bar."

Throat painfully knotted from the effort of holding back tears, she had to ask, "Do you? Love me?"

"A few minutes ago, I might've said yes. Now?" He shook his head. "Hell if I know."

MASON GAVE EACH girl a goodbye hug and kiss, whispering his love, but only when he stormed down to the garage, then careened out of the driveway behind the wheel of Alec's Hummer did he breathe.

What had just happened? Had he honestly taken the step his dad and Calder had advised, only to be summarily shot down?

He'd done everything for Hattie and her sister's girls. He'd been prepared to give up everything—including the career he credited with saving his life after Melissa's betrayal damn near killed him. He'd done all of that and for what?

Five minutes later, he reached his dad's only to find Fern's truck in the drive.

Swell.

Figured the one time he really needed to talk with his father, Jerry had more important matters on his mind. And here it wasn't even Saturday. Regardless, he rapped on the door until his old man answered.

"What're you doing?" his dad asked. "Everything all right with Hattie and the girls?"

Mason sighed. There wasn't a short version to the story, and since he was mortified about having his proposal shot down, he told a necessary white lie. "I, ah, got called in. It's short notice, but it comes with the territory."

"Hate seeing you go," Jerry said before pulling him into a tight hug. "But I sure am proud of you, son."

His dad would never know how much Mason needed

that affirmation—that he was on track in at least one portion of his life.

After saying goodbye to Fern, and getting a hug from her, too, Mason drove to the airport. His dad wanted him to stay with him until his flight, but Mason politely declined. He needed to be alone. Have time to think. At this time of night the airport terminal would be closed, but on his phone, he went ahead and made a reservation online to fly out first thing in the morning. He'd sleep in the car. His dad knew everyone, and promised Mason that if he left the vehicle's keys with airport security, he'd get it back to Hattie.

Most everything he owned was at the house, but screw it. Belongings were replaceable. Only thing he couldn't buy was a new heart.

HATTIE WOKE TO find her eyes swollen and red and an empty pillow alongside her instead of Mason resting his hand on her belly. The loss was crushing. The fact that she'd brought this pain on herself? Certifiable.

But what else could she have done?

Rolling over, she gripped the blanket, drawing it up to her chin. Where was he now? Maybe once he calmed from the initial shock of her frank rejection, he'd understand it was for the best.

But was it? Fear hanging heavy at the base of her stomach told a different story. What if turning him away for what she perceived to be all the right reasons turned out to be her life's single biggest mistake?

Over the baby monitor came the sound of Vivian's cries.

Before Hattie could pull on her robe and poke her cold toes into slippers, Vanessa had chimed in. Had it really only been yesterday Mason had helped her with the morn-

ing routine? She now wished she hadn't taken a moment
of his presence for granted.

He meant everything to her, but to be with him meant
destroying her family, which was already so badly broken.

"You're a sight for sore eyes."

"Thanks." Mason closed the door behind him and entered the apartment he shared with Cooper. Since their
friends Calder and Heath had married, they were the last
remaining bachelors on their SEAL team. Thanks to Hattie, Mason suspected he was done when it came to anything more than sharing a drink with the fairer sex. Ha!
Fairer sex, his ass. A more appropriate title would be that
women were the shortsighted, incapable-of-trust sex.

"Have a good holiday?" Cooper asked, pausing "Call
of Duty" on his Xbox.

"Swell."

"Me, too." Cooper had never been the overly talkative
type, and it looked as if he hadn't changed since Mason
had been gone. "Well, it's been a long day. Think I'll grab
a quick shower, then turn in."

"Sounds good, man. See you in the a.m."

"Well, if you ask me, I say good riddance." Hattie's mom
fanned a pile of scrapbooking paper while her father added
another log to their hearth's fire.

Hattie couldn't wrap her head around her parents' one-
eighty. Mason had been out of her life for a week, and the
second they'd heard through the Conifer gossip hotline that
he'd left town for good, they'd run right over to Melissa's
extending not only the mother of all olive branches, but
multiple offers to help with her nieces.

Just as Hattie feared, the girls were on the verge of being
inconsolable with Mason gone. Perpetually irritable and

weepy, they seemed like different babies from the ones they'd been only a short time ago.

Her dad jiggled Vanessa on his knee. "Me and my fist would like to claim credit for sending him on his way, but he's always been a smart kid. He no doubt finally got the clue he wasn't wanted around here."

"Would you two knock it off," Hattie snapped. When Vivian cried in her carrier, Hattie lifted her, pacing while trying to soothe the cranky infant. "This is Mason we're talking about. He's a longtime family friend who's helped me more times than I can count—and both of you. Look how his leaving has affected your granddaughters. When he was here, except for the first couple weeks after losing Melissa and Alec, they never acted like this."

Her mother slapped her craft papers to the coffee table. "So, you're saying your sister's memory was only worth two weeks?"

"I didn't mean that at all," Hattie said above Vivian's increased wails. "I just think that where Mason is concerned, you two are being disrespectful. Mason's a good guy—a great guy. I'm sorry he left." *All the more so, because a huge reason why I turned him away was out of respect for you.*

"SNOWMAN, MY THREE-YEAR-OLD girl runs faster than you! Get the lead out!"

"Yessir, Master Chief." In the week Mason had been back on the job, he'd sorely missed his peaceful days playing Mr. Mom. Soon enough, his body would be back in top-notch form, but he feared getting his head back in the right place may take longer.

When the team stopped running for a water break, Calder approached him. "You look like crap."

"Thanks, man. Love you, too."

"Thought you were going to marry the girl?"

"What gave you that dumbass idea?" Mason splashed half the contents of his water bottle over his head.

Calder checked to make sure they were alone, then said in a low tone, "I told you the secret. Remember? How *you'll know when you know.*"

After finishing off the water, Mason said, "Obviously, I didn't know."

EVEN TWO WEEKS after their latest argument, Hattie refused to leave her nieces with her parents, so she had them with her while cleaning out her old apartment. Trevor, a long-time bartender and friend, had stepped up so much when she'd broken her arm and after Mason had left that she'd promoted him to night manager. Along with the title, he'd be moving upstairs. At least he would as soon as all of her old junk was gone.

Hard to believe she'd once been such a pack rat.

Mason ran a tight ship. Living with him had taught her the benefits of streamlining her lifestyle.

She missed him with a gnawing, nagging pain that rarely went away. While she still couldn't be sure he hadn't proposed out of nostalgia for her sister or just plain old pity over not wanting her to be a single mom, she constantly second-guessed her decision.

If she'd said yes, would he be here with her now?

But would that have even been fair, considering how much he loved his job?

Vivian grew bored with her play mat and wasn't afraid to show it with a good old-fashioned tantrum. By the time Vanessa chimed in, Clementine charged up the stairs to check on the commotion.

She lifted a wide-eyed, sniffling Vivian for a hug and said, "Too many more screams like that, and you'll give Auntie Clem a heart attack."

"Sorry." Hattie calmed Vanessa. "I'm almost done. Just need to go through this box of purses."

"No worries." To Vivian, she said, "You're coming downstairs with me. It's about time you learned to appreciate cherries."

"Thanks," Hattie called after her friend.

Reaching far back into a cedar cabinet, she grabbed the last of the purses she was donating to charity. It was the black dress purse she'd carried the day she and Mason saw Benton for the reading of her sister's will.

She clutched the purse to her chest, willing herself not to cry.

"Van, we should've fought for him, huh? Told your nosy grandparents we don't care what they think."

THREE WEEKS LATER, while the girls "ran" wild in their walkers, Hattie was scooping ashes from the fireplace when her cell rang.

Even though Mason had his own assigned ring tone, she couldn't help wishing it'd somehow be him.

After wiping her hands on a rag, she grabbed her phone, only to swallow her usual disappointment upon seeing the caller wasn't Mason, but Benton—Melissa's lawyer.

"Hattie?"

"Yes… Hi. Are you making preparations to head out to your mine for the season?" She sat on the hearth, where she could keep an eye on the rowdy, shrieking twins.

"Not exactly. Do you have any free time today to stop by?"

"I—I suppose. Is everything okay?" Her stomach tightened. Had Alec's parents decided to contest the will?

"Oh, sure. Just stumbled across something I thought you might like to have."

AFTER A QUICK SHOWER, Hattie dropped the girls with her mom, then drove straight toward Benton's. Judging by the stacks of paperwork and folders lining his reception area, he'd been cleaning his office. Or maybe the better term would be *rearranging,* as it didn't appear he'd disposed of much—more like he'd moved it around.

"Benton?" Hattie called into the gloom, stepping gingerly around a few files that'd fallen.

"Back here!" he shouted from his office.

She found him under his desk, picking up paper clips. "Need help?"

"Nope. Just about got them all." He raised up, only to conk his head on the underside of the desk. He winced, rubbing the offended spot. "Guess I had that coming."

She sat on one of the folding chairs. "No one deserves that kind of pain. Hitting your head's the worst."

"Hold your judgment until after you see this." He held out a sealed envelope.

"What is it?"

"A letter—from Melissa. I guess the day you were all in here for the reading of her will, it must've fallen. I'm deeply sorry. I never even knew she'd stashed it in the packet."

Hattie held the letter in her trembling hands, and shock didn't begin to cover her myriad of emotions. Elation for the privilege of one, last message from her sister. Anger for Benton having been so careless as to have lost it. And honestly, a little trepidation as to what her sister had found so important to convey that she'd needed to share from beyond her grave.

"I'll leave you in private." He stumbled from the room, closing the door behind him.

For a few minutes, Hattie sat perfectly still.

Then she tore open the envelope, but struggled removing the contents as her hands refused to stop trembling. When she'd finally unfolded two pieces of the embossed stationery Melissa had ordered after her wedding, she read the dear words through tears.

Sweet Hattie—
If you're reading this, my premonitions have come true and Alec and I have gone to a better place. You may find it strange—me leaving my two angels to you and Mason—but to my way of thinking it was the most natural, honorable act I could've done.

I have to admit I was never the kind of woman Mason deserved. I was never good like you. You were always off helping someone while I pursued the perfect tan. In death, I guess I finally found the strength to admit I could be a little shallow—or, okay, maybe a lot!

Laughing along with her sister's spirit, Hattie brushed tears that refused to stop falling.

Before I seem too down on myself, let me reassure you that while I lacked in some areas, overall, I was the bomb. But, dear sister, so are you, which is why I want my girls raised by the kindest, sweetest, most gentle person I know. *You.*

Now, here's where Mason comes in. One of my greatest regrets was hurting him. I blamed him for being gone on long fishing trips as the cause of our breakup, but in all honesty, I couldn't stand being alone. That was never a life I wanted. Alec was always hosting parties and had his big, gorgeous house. I always wanted to be a real-life princess and Alec gave me that chance. In the end, I betrayed Mason and hurt him deeply.

You and Mason shared a connection I never had with him, even while we were married. Your friendship at times felt stronger than our supposed love. Looking back, I think I viewed him as a conquest, a trophy to be won. He's a good man who deserves good love—your love.

Hattie, please don't do anything stupid like let Mom and Dad dictate how you live your life. They mean well, but what I want for you and my children is to *live* well. As I'm writing this, I know I'm not long for this world. My dreams of dying scare me, but not as much as the thought of my girls growing up all alone. Who knows, maybe these crazy dreams are the result of too much wine and I'll live to be a hundred, but if not, with you as Vivian and Vanessa's mom, I know they'll be well cared for and loved. And if Mason sticks around, and you two finally realize how great you'd be together, then maybe I'll go to the spirit world in good favor.

Please raise my girls as much as possible in the old ways of cherishing children. It makes me happy to believe our family's spirits live on in them.

Finally, even if you don't find true love with Mason, please don't ever stop searching. You've always been the smarter of us two, but in this case, please don't overanalyze when it comes to love, but go where your heart guides you. When the time comes, you'll know what to do.

I adore you, dear sister. Please don't ever be sad when thinking of me. I pray you and my girls smile when saying my name, as I will do the same for all of you.

—M

Barely able to read the last part through tears, Hattie reached to Benton's desk for a tissue. How ironic was it that if she'd read this letter months ago, absorbing her sister's advice to follow her heart, she would have recognized what she now realized she'd instinctively known all along—Mason was, had always been, the right man for her.

Figuring it would do little good to beat herself up about letting him go, she instead chose a more proactive route to self-help by jumping headfirst after her dreams.

"LATELY, IT'S BEEN you asking me this," Mason said to Heath in between training dives, "but are you all right? You were out of it down there. It's not like you to space on your decompression time."

"I'm good." He bit into a power bar. "Aw, who am I trying to kid? Nothing could be further from the truth."

Mason leaned in closer. "What's wrong?"

"You know how Patricia and I have been trying for a baby? Turns out she hasn't been able to conceive because of a tumor."

Mason's stomach sank. Patricia was one of the nicest gals he'd ever known. "It's benign, though, right? She's gonna be okay?"

"Hope so. Don't know what I'd do without her."

Mason knew the feeling. Most days, being without Hattie and the girls felt akin to breathing with one lung.

Only out here on open water was he able to find some semblance of peace. Otherwise, he couldn't help wondering what she and the girls were doing. How many new things had the twins learned?

"Didn't mean to drag you down," Heath said. "I need to stay positive. I'm taking the rest of the week off to be with her during her tests."

"I'll be thinking of you both. Hopefully, she'll be fine."

"From your lips to God's ears…"

The rest of the day they were too busy for chitchat, but during what little downtime Mason did have, he couldn't help but think what a raw deal Heath and Patricia were getting. Here were two people who loved each other but, by a cruel twist of fate, may not have much more time together.

Conversely, he and Hattie might've had all the time in the world, but she'd thrown it away.

HATTIE GLANCED AT the address she'd typed into her phone's map feature, double-checking it against the real thing in front of her.

Tipsea's. This was the place.

"You ready for this, ladies?" Vivian and Vanessa ignored her in favor of grabbing for a butterfly that had made the mistake of entering the twins' air space. "Some help you two are."

She forced a deep breath of muggy, brine-laced air.

So far, she liked Virginia. The warmth of not only the temperature, but the people.

Summoning her every ounce of courage, Hattie yanked open the bar's door, intent on meeting Maggie.

"Let me get that for you," a naval-uniformed passerby offered when she struggled to fit the girls' stroller inside.

"Thanks. Guess this place wasn't designed to be kid friendly, huh?"

He laughed. "Not exactly, but have fun."

"Thanks." It took her eyes a while to adjust to the gloom. Whereas her bar had tons of windows overlooking the bay, Tipsea's provided a dim-lit hideaway for its patrons. Neon beer signs glowed from every wall and six pool tables were half-occupied in a gaming area. This early in the afternoon, the dance floor was empty, as were most of the tables and booths. Four men ringed the bar: two sat nursing their draft beers; the others played video games. The scent of beer and what would no doubt be a great cheeseburger flavored the air.

A slight woman with snow-white hair rounded the bar, holding out her arms for a hug. "You have to be Hattie."

Hattie laughed. "Did my posse give me away?"

"Just a smidge. Come on. Let's get y'all to the office. Hank!" she called to the bartender. "I'm headed to the back. Holler if you need me."

"Will do," he said with a wave and curious glance in Hattie's direction.

Hattie was pleasantly surprised to find Maggie's office to be a bright, homey retreat from what she'd seen so far.

"Thank you for agreeing to meet with me," she said once Maggie sat on a comfortable floral sofa.

Hattie had taken the matching armchair.

"My pleasure. I have to say, your offer took me off guard, but after thinking on it a bit, partial retirement does hold a certain appeal."

"I'm glad. If everything works out, this will hopefully launch an exciting new chapter for us both."

"I REALLY DON'T feel up to this," Mason complained to Cooper on their way to Tipsea's. It might be St. Patrick's Day, but all the green beer in the world wouldn't bring back his smile.

"Knock it off. You haven't left the apartment for anything other than work in weeks. A night out with the guys will do you good."

Wishing he'd driven himself so he'd have an escape vehicle, Mason shook his head, mumbling, "This is B.S. I'm too old to be kidnapped."

"Whatever. Just shut up and quit complaining. I promise, you'll have a great time."

The second Mason hit Tipsea's rowdy crowd, he attempted turning right back around to hail a cab, but Cooper grabbed hold of his arm. "Seriously, man. You need to head for the bar."

"Not thirsty."

"Hells bells…" Cooper tugged him past a dancing leprechaun and a blonde in a green bikini.

What did it say about Mason that he wasn't interested? He should've been over Hattie by now, but more than ever, he feared that day may never come. Cooper said, "Loosen up and at least try having a good time. Look—" he pointed toward the bar, where a smoking-hot brunette wore blinking, green antennae "—the bartender's giving away green shots."

Mason took another long look at the woman, a serious look, and then she met his stare and the shock of finding Hattie standing behind his favorite bar damn near had him swallowing his tongue.

"Is it really her?" he asked Cooper, even though his friend and Hattie had never even met.

"If you mean your girl, Hattie, according to Maggie it is. She threatened me bodily harm if I didn't bring you down here tonight." He waved to a few guys on another SEAL team. "Now that I'm done babysitting, have fun."

She said something to one of the other three bartenders on duty, then approached him. Her brown eyes shone with emotion. He wanted to say something smartassed that would show he didn't care she'd come to him, but how could he do that when he did care—more than anything.

In the middle of the crowded bar, he wrapped his arms around her, breathing her in. "I didn't know I was capable of missing a person like I've missed you."

"I feel the same," she said. "I'm sorry. I wanted to accept your proposal, but the whole time we were together, it felt like such a dream, I guess I never believed it could actually be true."

He kissed her and his world once again made sense. She tasted of strawberries and mint and that special something that always reminded him of her. "I never would've asked if I hadn't planned on spending the rest of my life with you and the girls. Speaking of which, where are they?"

"With friends of yours. Calder and Pandora. Maggie introduced me to them. She says Pandora works for the best child-care agency in town."

After a light shake of his head, he asked, "How is it you know all of my friends? How long have you been in town?"

"Only a week, but it felt like a lifetime without seeing you. Maggie and I are now partners. Clem and her mom are looking into buying my bar, and I rented out Melissa and Alec's house. I wanted to get settled here first—just in case you took wooing."

"What's that mean?"

She pressed her lips to his, teasing him with her wicked tongue. "You know, if you'd still been mad at me, I would've needed a job and house to retreat to. In your terms—a base of operations, because no matter what your response was to seeing me, from now until forever, you're mine."

"I like the sound of that." After more kissing and being jostled by the crowd, frustration got the better of him and

Mason found himself wanting Hattie all for himself. "Mind getting out of here?"

"Thought you'd never ask."

With Hattie's fingers interwoven with his, Mason led her out of the bar and into their new life, speechless and choked up over the realization that for once in his life, a woman he loved ran to him instead of away.

He never thought he'd believe it, but maybe Melissa's Inuit dreams had some substance to them after all.

Resting her head on his shoulder, Hattie softly sighed. "I love you. Pretty sure I've always loved you."

"I love you, Hat Trick—only I was too dumb to realize it until it was almost too late." From the front pocket of his jeans, he withdrew the ring he'd carried with him every day since leaving. "Before we go a step further— marry me?"

She feigned taking a moment to think about it.

"Not funny," he said with a growl and kiss. "Answer, or I may rescind the offer."

"Yes. Of course." Arms around him, fingers raking his hair, her lips confirmed her words.

"That's better." He slipped on her ring, kissed her finger, then asked, "Where are we going?"

"I thought you knew? My rental car's back at the bar."

Tilting his head back, he groaned. "I wish you'd have said something a block earlier. We could've already been back at my apartment doing naughty things." He paused to whisper some of the specifics he'd been dreaming of for weeks.

Even the shadowy streetlights couldn't hide her blush. "That's awfully presumptuous, sailor. You really gonna talk to your future wife like that?"

He winked. "Every night—mornings, too, if the girls aren't up too early."

"Oh—well, in that case, we should probably get moving. We have a lot of lost time to make up for."

"You read my mind. How's the leg room in the backseat of your car?"

She laughed. "For what you have in mind, we're gonna need a model upgrade."

"Bummer. Guess if I've waited this long, though, a few more minutes won't kill me."

"Speak for yourself. Come on." Hattie ducked into the lobby of a boutique hotel, booked a room, then reacquainted herself with every inch of Mason's delicious body. Gone were all of her feelings of awkwardness and mistrust, replaced by a confidence she viewed as the greatest gift he'd ever given.

Sure, her ring was pretty, but most gorgeous of all was the way Mason made her feel inside and out. He'd changed everything about her for the better, and if it took the next sixty or so years, she'd spend every day of the rest of her life thanking him.

Epilogue

Hattie hadn't believed she'd find an even larger group of friends outside of Conifer, but she couldn't have been more wrong.

Dancing barefoot on the beach in celebration of her and Mason's June wedding were not only her new favorites like Calder and Pandora, Maggie, Heath and Patricia and Cooper, but even her old crowd who had flown in for the happy occasion. Of course, Fern and Jerry, along with Clementine, Joey and Dougie, as well as Clementine's mom. The most surprising guests of all were Hattie's parents.

At first, they'd stayed on the fringe of the celebration, but the longer the night went on, the more they joined in.

"Mind if I steal you and the groom for a sec?" Her dad took her hand, then shockingly reached for Mason's. With tears in his eyes, Lyle said, "I owe you both an apology. L-losing Melissa was the toughest thing I've ever been through. Mason, I hope one day you can forgive me for allowing my grief to drown my common sense. Hitting you was deplorable—especially when I now see how much joy you bring my sweet, beautiful Hattie." He paused a moment to collect himself. "Anyway, I don't mean to go on all night, but I also want to thank you both. Hattie, even when we didn't deserve it, you kept reminding your mom and I about how much we still had left to live for. Mason, no matter what, you've always been the true definition of a gentleman. I couldn't dream of anyone I'd rather have watching over my daughter."

"The honor's all mine, sir."

Both men embraced.

And then Akna joined in on the hugs.

But then, just in case the night grew too maudlin, Jerry and Fern were on hand, providing them all with their usual antics.

"You can't put that in there," Fern said when her husband slipped his bowl of ice cream into the chocolate fountain.

"I don't see why not. How else am I s'posed to get chocolate syrup on my scoop of vanilla?"

"You're impossible," Fern declared. "I can't take you anywhere."

"Like you're such a prize?" He appraised her full-skirted, purple-striped dress, yellow pumps and Shirley Temple curls. "What am I saying? Woman, you're the hottest thing west of the Mississippi—or I guess tonight that'd be east. Come on over here and give your Big Daddy a kiss."

Hiding her laugh against her new husband's chest, Hattie could scarcely contain her happiness. Even the girls seemed to be having a great time, flirting up a storm with Calder and Pandora's son.

"Back when we were in grade school," she said, "could you ever imagine our lives would turn out like this?"

"Honestly, at the time, I was more driven by schemes of how to nab the cookies from your lunch bag." He caressed her belly. "But now that I not only have you, *and* all of your future lunch treats, I am pretty psyched to see what our future holds."

Heart pounding from having kept her tiny secret for

three months, she asked, "What if I told you your hand is currently resting on our future?"

After taking a moment to process her words, his smile lit the night. "For real? You're pregnant?"

She nodded. "Is that okay?"

"Okay?" He lifted her only to swing her around and around. "It's perfection."

Funny he should choose that word, because she'd spent so much time working toward making everything in her life perfect. However, the one thing she'd learned from all of her attempts was that it wasn't possible. Only with Mason by her side, turned out perfection had been within reach all along. All it had taken was following her sister's sage advice to "go where your heart guides you."

In Hattie's case, that meant walking straight into her handsome SEAL's loving arms.

* * * * *

Be sure to look for the next book
in the OPERATION: FAMILY *series*
by Laura Marie Altom!
Available in 2014
wherever Harlequin books are sold.

#1481 HER CALLAHAN FAMILY MAN
Callahan Cowboys
Tina Leonard

When Jace Callahan and Sawyer Cash engaged in their secretive affair, neither of them anticipated an unplanned pregnancy. Jace wants to seal the deal with a quickie marriage...but it turns out he has a very reluctant bride!

#1482 MARRYING THE COWBOY
Blue Falls, Texas
Trish Milburn

When a tornado rips through Blue Falls, good friends Elissa Mason and Pete Kayne find themselves sharing a house. Suddenly Elissa is thinking about her *pal* in a whole new way....

#1483 THE SURPRISE HOLIDAY DAD
Safe Harbor Medical
Jacqueline Diamond

Adrienne Cavill delivers other women's babies, but can't have one of her own. Now she may lose the nephew she's raising, and her heart, to his long-absent father, Wade Hunter. Unless the two of them can come up with a different arrangement?

#1484 RANCHER AT RISK
Barbara White Daille

Ryan Molloy's job is running his boss's ranch, so he doesn't have time to babysit Lianne Ward. She's there to establish a boys' camp—and definitely doesn't need Ryan looking over her shoulder every minute!

REQUEST YOUR FREE BOOKS!
2 FREE NOVELS PLUS 2 FREE GIFTS!

HARLEQUIN®

American ★ Romance®

LOVE, HOME & HAPPINESS

YES! Please send me 2 FREE Harlequin® American Romance® novels and my 2 FREE gifts (gifts are worth about $10). After receiving them, if I don't wish to receive any more books, I can return the shipping statement marked "cancel." If I don't cancel, I will receive 4 brand-new novels every month and be billed just $4.74 per book in the U.S. or $5.24 per book in Canada. That's a savings of at least 14% off the cover price! It's quite a bargain! Shipping and handling is just 50¢ per book in the U.S. and 75¢ per book in Canada.* I understand that accepting the 2 free books and gifts places me under no obligation to buy anything. I can always return a shipment and cancel at any time. Even if I never buy another book, the two free books and gifts are mine to keep forever.

154/354 HDN F4YN

Name _____ (PLEASE PRINT) _____

Address _____ Apt. # _____

City _____ State/Prov. _____ Zip/Postal Code _____

Signature (if under 18, a parent or guardian must sign) _____

Mail to the Harlequin® Reader Service:
IN U.S.A.: P.O. Box 1867, Buffalo, NY 14240-1867
IN CANADA: P.O. Box 609, Fort Erie, Ontario L2A 5X3

Want to try two free books from another line?
Call 1-800-873-8635 or visit www.ReaderService.com.

* Terms and prices subject to change without notice. Prices do not include applicable taxes. Sales tax applicable in N.Y. Canadian residents will be charged applicable taxes. Offer not valid in Quebec. This offer is limited to one order per household. Not valid for current subscribers to Harlequin American Romance books. All orders subject to credit approval. Credit or debit balances in a customer's account(s) may be offset by any other outstanding balance owed by or to the customer. Please allow 4 to 6 weeks for delivery. Offer available while quantities last.

Your Privacy—The Harlequin® Reader Service is committed to protecting your privacy. Our Privacy Policy is available online at www.ReaderService.com or upon request from the Harlequin Reader Service.

We make a portion of our mailing list available to reputable third parties that offer products we believe may interest you. If you prefer that we not exchange your name with third parties, or if you wish to clarify or modify your communication preferences, please visit us at www.ReaderService.com/consumerchoice or write to us at Harlequin Reader Service Preference Service, P.O. Box 9062, Buffalo, NY 14269. Include your complete name and address.

HAR13R

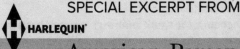
*Their families may be rivals, but Jace Callahan
just can't stay away from Sawyer Cash!*

Jace Callahan appeared to be locked in place, thunderstruck. What had him completely poleaxed was that the little darling who had such spunk was quite clearly as pregnant as a busy bunny in spring.

She made no effort to hide it in a curve-hugging hot pink dress with long sleeves and a high waist. Taupe boots adorned her feet, and she looked sexy as a goddess, but for the glare she wore just for him.

A pregnant Sawyer Cash was a thorny issue, especially since she was the niece of their Rancho Diablo neighbor, Storm Cash. The Callahans didn't quite trust Storm, in spite of the fact that they'd hired Sawyer on to bodyguard the Callahan kinder.

But then Sawyer had simply vanished off the face of the earth, leaving only a note of resignation behind. No forwarding address, a slight that he'd known was directed at him.

Jace knew this because for the past year he and Sawyer had had "a thing," a secret they'd worked hard to keep completely concealed from everyone.

He'd missed sleeping with her these past many months she'd elected to vacate Rancho Diablo with no forwarding address. Standing here looking at her brought all the familiar desire back like a screaming banshee.

Yet clearly they had a problem. Best to face facts right up front. "Is that why you went away from Rancho Diablo?" he asked, pointing to her tummy.

She raised her chin. "It won't surprise me if you back out, Jace. You were never one for commitment."

Commitment, his boot. Of his six siblings, consisting of one sister and five brothers, he'd been the one who'd most longed to settle down.

He gazed at her stomach again, impressed by the righteous size to which she'd grown in the short months since he'd last seen her—and slept with her.

He wished he could drag her to his bed right now.

"I'm your prize, beautiful," he said with a grin. "No worries about that."

Look for HER CALLAHAN FAMILY MAN,
by USA TODAY bestselling author Tina Leonard
next month, from Harlequin® American Romance®.